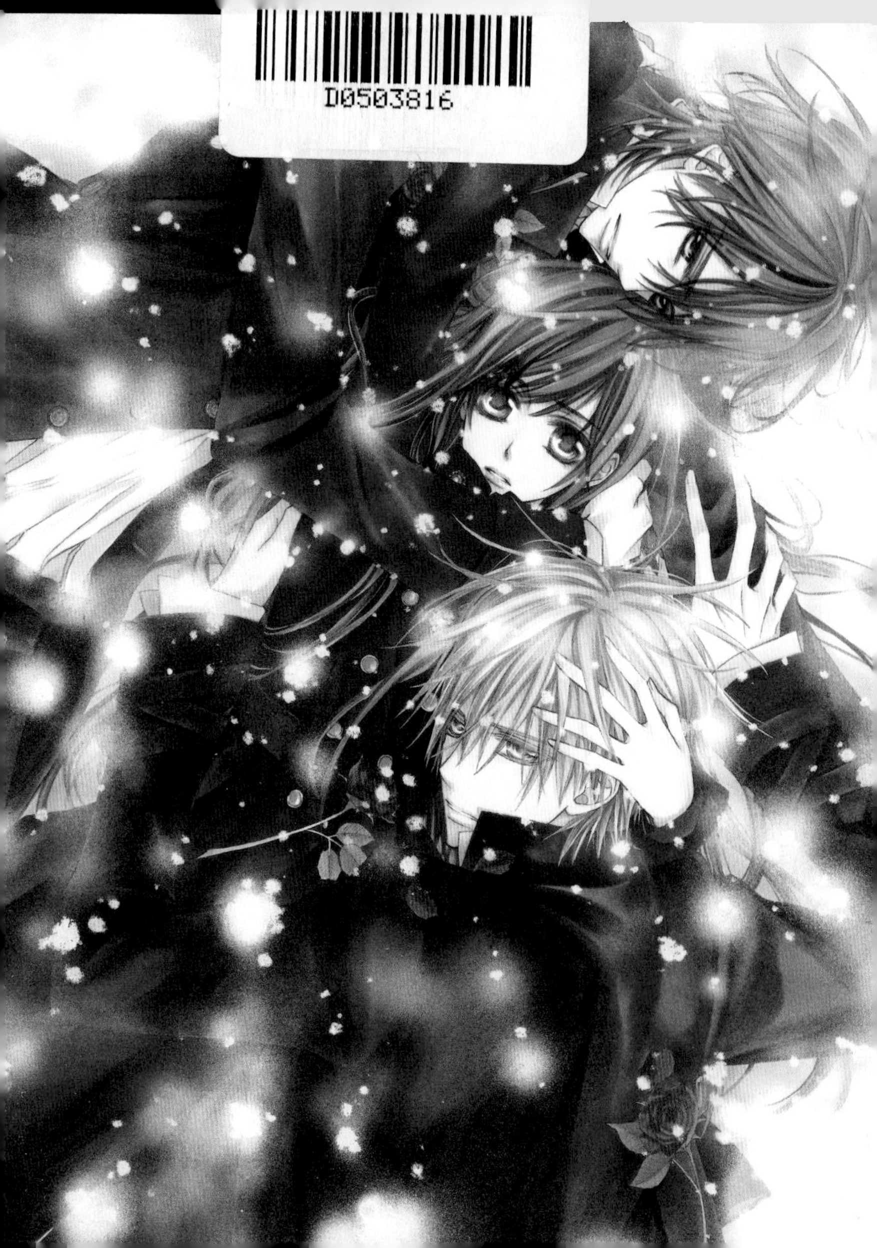

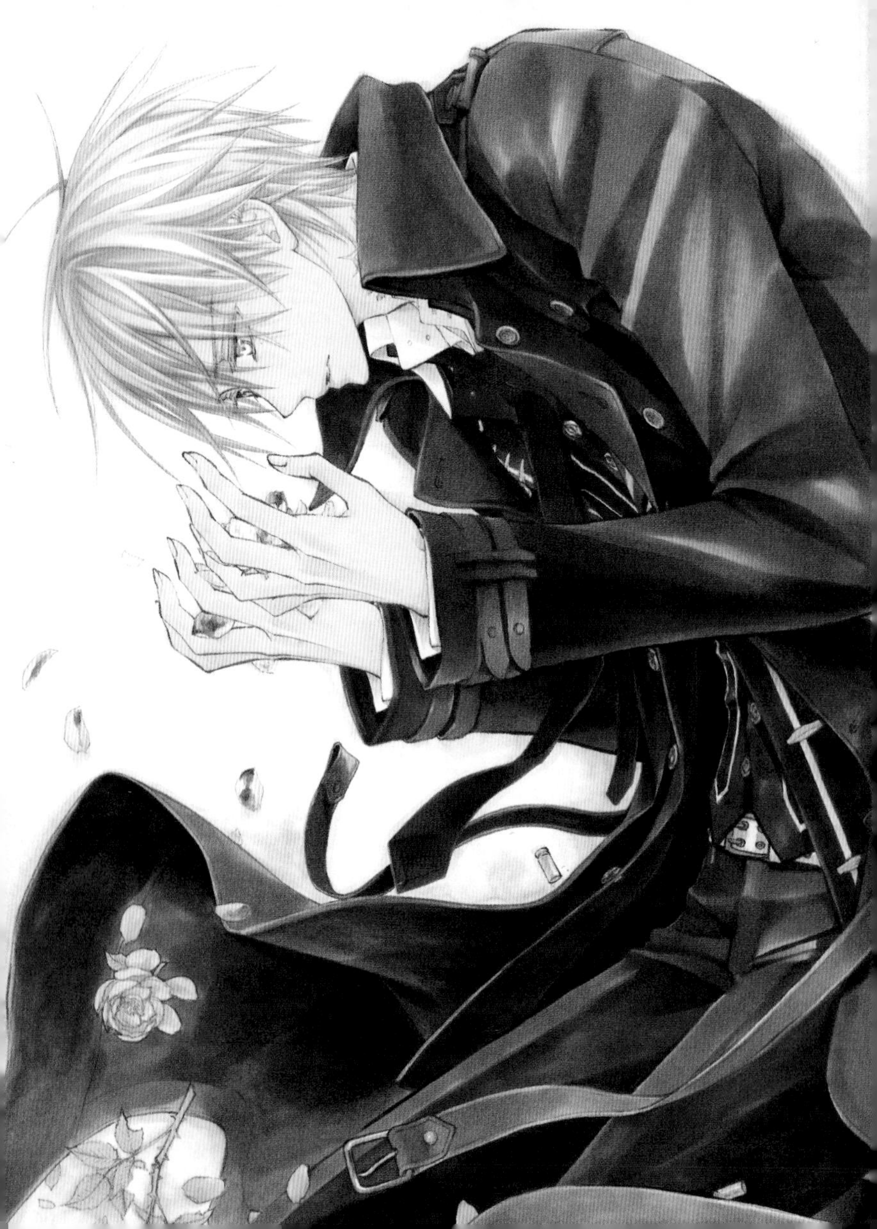

VAMPIRE KNIGHT

FLEETING DREAMS

Vampire Knight: Fleeting Dreams

Vampire Knight Frail No Yume
by Matsuri Hino / Ayuna Fujisaki

© Matsuri Hino / Ayuna Fujisaki 2013
All rights reserved.
First published in Japan in 2013 by HAKUSENSHA, Inc., Tokyo.
English language translation rights arranged with HAKUSENSHA, Inc., Tokyo.

Cover Illustration by **Matsuri Hino**
Design by **Fawn Lau**
Edited by **Nancy Thistlethwaite**

A Shojo Beat Novel
Published by
VIZ Media, LLC
P.O. Box 77010
San Francisco, CA 94107

www.shojobeat.com

Library of Congress Cataloging-in-Publication Data
Fujisaki, Ayuna.
 [Short stories. Selections]
 Vampire knight : fleeting dreams / created by Matsuri Hino ; written by Ayuna Fujisaki ;
translated by Su Mon Han.
    pages cm
 "A Shojo Beat novel."
 First published in Japan in 2013 by Hakusensha under title: Vampire knight frail no yume.
 ISBN 978-1-4215-7728-9 (paperback)
 1. Love stories, Japanese—Translations into English. 2. Vampires—Fiction. [1. Love—Fiction. 2.
Vampires—Fiction.] I. Hino, Matsuri. II. Han, Su Mon. III. Title. IV. Title: Fleeting dreams.
 PZ7.F95136Vam 2014
 [Fic]—dc23
                    2014033774

Printed in the U.S.A.
First printing, December 2014
Second printing, July 2019

Shojo Beat

VAMPIRE KNIGHT

FLEETING DREAMS

Created by
Matsuri Hino

Written by
Ayuna Fujisaki

Translated by Su Mon Han

A Shojo Beat Novel

Yuki Cross
The princess of the Kuran clan. She has regained all her lost memories and powers. She is the adopted daughter of Headmaster Cross.

Takuma Ichijo
Vampire aristocrat. Grandson of Ichio, the most influential vampire in the senate. Takuma has parted ways with Kaname and now aligns his actions with Sara's.

Akatsuki Kain
Vampire aristocrat. He has the power to manipulate fire.

Ruka Souen
A vampire aristocrat with the power to generate illusions. She has been friends with Akatsuki Kain and Hanabusa Aido since childhood.

Seiren
The most loyal of Kaname's followers. She can silently appear out of nowhere.

Hanabusa Aido
Vampire aristocrat. He has the power to freeze matter. He is currently staying with the Kurans to oversee Yuki's education.

CHARACTERS

Zero Kiryu
Vampire hunter. He became a vampire after being bitten by a pureblood. Zero and Yuki went their separate ways once she returned to living as a pureblood.

Kaname Kuran
Yuki's adopted brother and her betrothed. He has been watching over Yuki her entire life. He is the progenitor of the pureblood Kuran clan.

Asato Ichijo
Known as "Ichio," he is Takuma's grandfather and the head of the vampire senate.

Sara Shirabuki
A pureblood. She secretly murdered Ouri, her fiancé.

Rido Kuran
Yuki's uncle. He has an extremely strong attachment to his younger sister Juri.

Headmaster Cross
The headmaster of Cross Academy. His aim is for humans and vampires to coexist peacefully.

Kaito Takamiya
A vampire hunter. Upon Yagari's recommendation, he has begun work as a teacher at Cross Academy.

Toga Yagari
An extremely powerful vampire hunter. He is the one who trained Zero and Kaito.

Sayori Wakaba
Yuki's best friend. She is concerned about Yuki, whose whereabouts appear to be unknown.

Kasumi Kageyama
Class representative at Cross Academy. He has a crush on Ruka.

Rima Toya
Vampire aristocrat. She works with Shiki as a model.

Senri Shiki
A fairly taciturn vampire aristocrat. He works as a model.

CONTENTS

DERANGED
LOVE

"Why won't you love me, Juri?"

This girl has the same scent as Juri.

As I stand close to her, feeling her warmth, I gradually notice my pulse slowing. The point of Yuki's scythe protrudes from my chest.

That's right, this is the weapon that Juri's daughter wields...

Why must it always be this way? Why does my heart's desire always slip through my fingers? As my mind begins to fade, deep in my heart, I call out my love's name.

Juri...!

Deep red blood stained my hands.

Glancing down, I saw two great piles of ash spreading slowly across the floor. This was all that remained of my parents.

"That's what you get for getting in my way, you naughty things..."

My parents had taken my precious Juri far away from me, had made it so we could never meet. Worse yet, they had betrothed me to another without even a thought to my consent. The one they had chosen was Shizuka Hio, a pureblood princess who was still but a tiny child.

"I understand that to protect our unsullied bloodline, I must wed a pureblood vampire...But must it be this child?"

"Is there some other girl you have in mind?"

I looked into Mother's suspicious eyes and smiled broadly.

"Of course there is. You know I'm in love with her, don't you?"

"That's the one match we cannot approve of," Father's deep voice interjected, his eyes hard upon me.

"Why not? I simply can't understand what objections you could have to our match. You know how precious she is to me. Yes...So very precious that I want to devour her..."

The memory of her clear gaze and silken skin rose unbidden in my mind. I felt my eyes widen with pleasure, once again caught in her enchantment.

Catching my expression, Father cast a disgusted look at me. "That love of yours is perverse."

"Perverse?"

I, perverse?

At my astonished look, Father muttered heavily, "In any case, the best thing for you both is to keep you apart from Juri."

In that moment, a dark fire flared up in my chest. I suddenly understood what it was Father meant. I was completely swayed by the basest of vampire instincts to their unsightly extreme. That was why I desired the one linked to me by blood.

My own sister.

But in that case, what could possibly be wrong with our union? I loved Juri and no other. She who could never sully another person. She was my sanctuary, my hallowed ground.

"You will join yourself to the Hio princess. I won't hear another word of protest."

Those words wound up being the very last Father ever spoke.

Even now I can still vividly recall the day of Juri's birth.

"Rido-sama! Haruka-sama! The baby has been born!"

We rushed straight for the room in which the baby had been delivered. When we entered, there lay Mother upon the bed, her face weary but beaming.

"Our house has been blessed with its first little princess," she said. Mother looked so happy, her lips curved in a smile as she gazed down at the tiny baby asleep beside her. "Rido,

Haruka, come see your little sister's darling face."

At that, my younger brother Haruka stepped forward and peered intently at this new, tiny existence so recently come into the world. As for myself, I will confess that newborns seemed very uninteresting to me at the time. However...

"Come now, Rido-sama. See how adorable your little sister is."

At our nanny's insistence, I wound up holding my newborn sister in my arms. Unable as the baby was to yet lift up her head, she sprawled awkwardly in my arms. Fearing that I would drop her, I instinctively drew her tightly against me. Held there against my chest, the baby quieted, and for a moment, I thought she smiled up at me.

It was in that moment that—somewhere in the depths of my being—something abruptly flared to life. What was it? What was this sudden rush of exhilaration? I was overwhelmed by the urge to devour her. I clung desperately to rational thought to prevent myself from losing control.

She is not ripe yet. Not yet...

I pressed my lips softly to the baby's cheek. That was the greatest expression of love I was capable of mustering. Unbeknownst to me then, the tender softness of that cheek had put me under its enchantment.

"Rido, you seem to have taken a shine to your little sister."

"But of course. Because this girl is my most precious darling."

"Rido, you're..."

For some reason, Mother's face appeared rather shaken. I looked into her anxious eyes and smiled broadly.

"It's all right. She's going to be mine someday, so I'll be sure to keep her safe."

And so the new addition to the family was given the name Juri. I loved Juri from the very depths of my heart, and I spent my every waking moment with her. Though Mother would tell me repeatedly to let Nanny see to her needs, the idea of leaving Juri in her care simply didn't sit well with me. The very idea of an outsider laying hands on Juri disgusted me. In all honesty, I didn't even like other members of my family touching her.

As she grew older, I often took Juri out for strolls in our garden. On one particular night the moon was especially bright, and the air was lush with the heady scent of red roses in full bloom.

"Rido, don't the roses smell wonderful?"

"Indeed they do."

I plucked a beautiful rose blossom from its stem and turned to show it to Juri. Doing so, I pricked my fingertip on a sharp thorn. Crimson blood began pooling upon it. Unable to completely suppress my instincts, I smeared my blood upon Juri's lips.

"Juri, this is my blood. Do you understand how much I love you? You should know the taste of my blood. Know it so well that you will never learn to desire another's."

Juri gazed up at me with wide, confused eyes.

"Rido, what are you doing?!" Mother rushed toward us,

striking my cheek and pulling Juri away from me to rob me of her. It was the first time Mother had ever hit me. But what stunned me more was the sensation of having Juri ripped from my side.

"Mother?"

"I'm sorry. But from now on, I do not want you to be alone with Juri."

Thereafter I stopped being able to spend as much time as I truly wished with Juri. My younger brother Haruka suffered no such restriction, so why should I have?

However, I never allowed my true emotions to show upon my face. I knew that if I expressed what I truly felt, it would only cause my parents to become even more wary of me. This took a monumental amount of self-control on my part, but I managed to behave myself. And anyway, I had plenty of time to wait them out. I could wait centuries upon centuries, into eternity itself.

But then, there came the day when everything crumbled. Yes, the day when my parents decided whom I was to marry.

It was really all Mother and Father's fault. I had been so very good. I had controlled myself for so long, and despite that they went ahead and entered into an agreement! How could I possibly forgive them for that?

I wonder why I suddenly remember all of that now. I have never been such a fool as to allow myself to wallow in sentimentality.

But just recalling Juri's warmth, her scent, and her velvety skin...Once again the feverish passion I haven't felt in so long is bubbling straight from the depths of me.

Juri...

How many times have I called that name now? Has there ever been another woman in this world so persistently pursued?

Juri, why wouldn't you be mine?

From the moment I had held the newborn Juri in my arms, I had meant never to let her go. So why is it that since that time

I remained in the place farthest from her? I, who loved and yearned for her more than any other?

When I heard the news that Juri was with child, I was filled with both a desperation to believe it untrue and a dark hatred for Haruka. It made me realize something. Juri and Haruka's child would be a pureblood, and his blood would house great power.

I felt my true nature rising within me as a smile lit my lips.

That is very interesting...

It would be the perfect way to gain power far beyond Haruka's. Darkness spread in my heart.

But in my lust for power, I wound up losing what was most precious to me.

How could anyone understand how lonesome and dull a world without Juri has been for me? The very act of drawing breath has become burdensome, and each moment in this new world brings me nothing but pain. Tell me, what meaning could there possibly be for me to exist in such a place?

What was it about me that she found so lacking?

The answer escapes me to this day, and I shall probably spend all the rest of eternity not knowing.

I force a last surge of strength into my arms as they encircle Yuki.

"What do I lack? How can I make you love me?"

"..."

I feel Yuki gasp softly.

This girl has the same scent as Juri...

To think that Juri—whom I can never touch or feel again— is here in my arms once more. If the price I must pay for this miracle is death, it doesn't seem so very bad an exchange.

"I...I love you so much that I want to devour you..."

I lay one hand over Yuki's wrist and brush the other along the nape of her neck. In that moment, the blade embedded in my chest stabs deeper into me.

"Juri..."

As my mind fades, I allow my thoughts to drift at will, seeking Juri.

My vision is hazy, and all sense of pain has left me entirely.

"Your weapon isn't what I want..."

In the next moment, a monstrous tangle of thorns and bramble envelops my body. Through the gaps where the enormous, innumerable thorns crisscross, fall a few long, silken strands of hair. They are a deep warm brown, just like Juri's.

I lift my hand and touch her hair, to touch her cheek. With this I can finally rejoin my love. I take my leave from this bleak and bitter world at last.

GIFTS
FOR
YUKI

A faint scent of roses wafted through the living room. Savoring the feeling of comfort the scent brought him, Kaname let his crimson eyes fall half closed in pleasure. Rose tea—gleaming a deep ruby red in its cup—had become a favorite of his recently.

"What is Yuki up to?"

"Yuki-sama is currently attending to her studies."

Kaname gave a slight nod of thanks in reply to Seiren, who was standing unobtrusively near her master.

"I see..."

Outside the window, there was nothing but the darkness of

night. It was the hour of greatest clarity for vampires.

"It's a bit past the time she was scheduled to stop. Though if she's become that dedicated to her studies, I suppose it's a good thing." Kaname replaced his teacup on its saucer without it making even the smallest sound.

Meanwhile, in Yuki's study room...

Aido's been frowning pretty hard for a while now. I guess my work still isn't good enough...

As Aido continued staring down at Yuki's answer sheet, his furrowed brow crinkled further. Throwing anxious glances at his profile, Yuki stood with her hands clasped anxiously before her as though in prayer.

I felt like I did really well on it too, she thought glumly. She had just completed a pop quiz covering various topics.

Since she had come to live in this grand house—the main Kuran residence in which she had been born—and Aido had begun overseeing her studies as her tutor, Yuki's mind had been in a despairing state. She found herself often thinking, *I don't even know what I don't understand anymore.* From such a state, she had relearned everything from the basics on up, and her efforts had begun to pay off little by little. Lately Yuki found that after reviewing her notes for the day, she understood enough to be able to prepare for the following day's lessons. Still...

Maybe I really am just that hopelessly dumb...If I still can't learn anything after all this, there's probably no hope for me outside of somehow turning back time and making better choices in life...

Feeling as though she were standing in a pit of quicksand and sinking despite her struggles, Yuki stared blankly at Aido's fingertips as they traced slowly down the column of answers. He checked each one carefully.

"I don't believe this," Aido mumbled suddenly. Yuki jumped at the sound of his voice.

I guess I did blow it. I'm sorry, Kaname-sama. I really am a lost cause! Teary-eyed, Yuki began a fervent litany of apologies in her heart to Kaname when Aido suddenly spoke again.

"I seriously don't believe it!" he muttered, making a check

mark with a sharp flick of his red pen to mark the column correct.

Huh? Blinking in surprise, Yuki watched in amazement as Aido's pen continued down the entire column, marking each answer correct.

"Correct...and so is this one! And this one! And this!"

Finally, he reached the last answer in the column and drew a large check above it. Yuki's eyes grew wide.

"Aido...does this mean...?"

"Yes." At the top of the answer sheet beside the name slot where Yuki had written her name, Aido scrawled a large "100%," and underlined it twice. "You got a perfect score."

Altogether too familiar with Yuki's terrible track record with test scores, Aido himself looked as though he'd witnessed a miracle.

"This too must be the fruits of my great and arduous labors as your tutor. Ah, the road was long..." Aido said, giving an exaggerated sigh and pretending to wipe sweat from his brow.

Yuki stared at the sheet, too shocked to process the large "100%" at the top. When at last the realization sank in, she shrieked, "I can't believe it! A perfect score! A perfect score! Kaname-sama, I finally got a perfect score!"

Clutching the answer sheet in her hands, Yuki leapt from her seat and dashed out of the room.

"What?! Not even so much as a thank-you for your diligent tutor?" he yelled behind her as she scurried out the study room door. Catching sight of her back as she ran down the hall, Aido couldn't help but chuckle.

"I can't believe she's so happy about her score. Unless..."

Unless she's never before received a perfect score on any test in her life?!

The faint scent of roses lingered in the elegant living room, but the refined atmosphere of the place was summarily shattered by the arrival of Yuki, frantically brandishing an answer sheet in her hand.

"Kaname-sama! I have something to show you!"

"What are you so worked up over, Yuki?" Kaname asked, a faint smile on his lips as he lifted his teacup to his lips. Watching him, Yuki quickly reined in her excitement.

"I-I'm sorry for disturbing you while you're resting," she said, flushing red with embarrassment at having bounded in like a cavorting child.

"There's no need to be so formal," Kaname said, setting his cup back upon its saucer and fixing her with a keen look. "By the way, Yuki, how long do you intend to continue calling me 'Kaname-sama'?"

Kaname had already mentioned that he preferred that Yuki call him simply by his first name. But Yuki felt hesitant to address him without any sort of honorific. She was still trying to get used to calling him just "Kaname," but she had forgotten to in her excitement.

"I'm sorry...K-Kaname," she apologized earnestly. His smile

softened, indicating that he was satisfied.

"Now then, what is it that has you so excited? You look so pleased. Something nice must have happened."

"Oh—yes! Actually, I...I scored 100 percent on my test today!" Yuki held the slightly rumpled sheet of paper toward him. "Ta-dah!" Feeling her cheeks reddening all of a sudden, Yuki quickly raised the paper to eye-level to hide her blush. The bright red "100%" Aido had scrawled at the top of the page all but glowed.

"I see. Congratulations, Yuki. You've worked very hard."

"Y-yes! Thank you so much, Kaname-sama—I mean, Kaname! I almost can't believe it myself!"

"You're the type of girl who can do anything you set your mind to, Yuki," Kaname said, his resonant voice smooth in Yuki's ears. He took the proffered sheet and carefully read over each answer. Looking satisfied, he said aloud, "Seiren, do you have a pen?"

"Of course, Kaname-sama," she answered, slipping a red

pen into his outstretched hand.

Flipping the pen elegantly over his long fingers into writing position, Kaname drew a large spiral surrounded by a circle of curlicues—the flower mark teachers sometimes drew on students' work to denote a job well done.

"Now you've got a flower mark from me too. Yuki, keep on doing your best."

"I will. I'll do my very best! Thank you."

Yuki took the test sheet back from him and held it close to her chest as though it were something precious. It was a darling sight. Kaname gazed at her and smiled softly.

Next Night

Huh?

Yuki woke to the scent of flowers. Rubbing her drowsy eyes, she slowly sat up in her bed and gazed around her room. There were flowers, flowers, and more flowers on every open surface. The room was so packed with blossoms that, for a moment, Yuki wondered if she hadn't hallucinated that she was in a flower field somewhere. There were roses in red, white, yellow, pink, and orange alongside white baby's breath, lilies, orchids, and daisies. It was impossible to say just how many flowers filled the room.

"W-why are all these flowers in my room?" Yuki wondered aloud. Still dumbfounded as she gazed around the room, when she made to slide out of the bed, she found a dear little bouquet on her bedside table. Attached to the bouquet was a small card with writing on it.

Congratulations on your perfect score. —Kaname

"All this is to celebrate my test score from yesterday?!"

Throwing a shawl over her nightgown, Yuki hurried from her room and nearly ran into Seiren in the hallway.

"Oh! Seiren! Do you know where Kaname-sama—I mean, where my brother is?"

"Kaname-sama stepped out just a short while ago."

"Oh..."

"More pressingly, Yuki-sama, while it is unobjectionable in the privacy of your own bed chamber, your current state of undress is..." Seiren arched an eyebrow, giving her nightgown a pointed look.

"Oh...Yes, I see. I just kind of rushed out..."

Drawing her shawl close to her chest, Yuki quickly retreated back into her bedroom.

The rest of the day passed uneventfully.

*I wonder when Kaname will come home...*Yuki thought. She wanted to thank him for the flowers and waited eagerly for his return. However, as the hours wore on, she nodded off into sleep.

Next Night

Huh?

Having just awoken, Yuki again blinked blankly at the

sight around her. The room was packed with flowers, flowers, and more flowers just as it had been the previous day. But in addition to that, there was now a towering pile of brightly wrapped presents adorned with elaborate ribbons in one corner of her room.

What is it this time?

Wrapping her shawl around her, Yuki crept timidly toward the bundle of presents. Sitting atop the stack was another card.

In honor of your hard work. —Kaname

"..."

Yuki tentatively took a small package from the pile and opened it. Inside was chocolate that had been shaped into an adorable baby chick. The chick was perfectly round and the color of eggshells. Its little eyes were made of dots of milk chocolate.

"Why a baby chick? Actually, why chocolate?" Yuki wondered aloud.

A quiet knock sounded on her door, and with a quiet, "I beg your pardon," Seiren entered. She glanced at the pile of presents and noted Yuki's hesitant grin.

"Kaname-sama delivered these to your room personally."

The image of Kaname merrily carrying piles of presents into her room and stacking them up in the corner as though he were a child playing with blocks—all the while careful so as not to wake her—was too much for Yuki. She groaned and rubbed her forehead.

"Incidentally, while he was arranging those boxes, Kaname-sama mentioned there are many ingredients in chocolate that are good for the brain."

"I-I see."

Setting aside the peculiar fixation vampires seemed to have with chocolate, Yuki then thought, *What is he thinking? Now I feel like I have tons of pressure on me to do well!*

With an unsteady smile, Yuki returned the baby chick-shaped chocolate to its box.

Next Night

My curtains have been replaced?

They had in fact been replaced by a new and expensive-look-ing set of curtains elaborately embroidered with blue roses.

And here I thought he'd be out of gifts for me by the third night.

Yuki decided she had been naïve. But to think he would come at her with the gift of a room makeover was original.

On the other hand, it was very like Kaname to forego stereo-typical gifts like fancy accessories and lavish dresses that would normally have come next. It seemed he had remembered that wearing sophisticated gowns made Yuki feel awkward and shy.

That said, while she could accept gifts of flowers and choc-olates gladly, now that he was buying actual room furnishings for her, Yuki was definitely beginning to feel awkward.

What's that?

Glancing around the room and ignoring the wall-to-wall flowers and mountain of chocolate, Yuki's eyes settled on yet another bundle of presents. The boxes were much bigger than the ones that had held the chocolate. Selecting one gift box, Yuki opened it to find a pillowcase. It was a pale blue and seemed to be part of a set with the blue rose curtains.

Surely these couldn't all be pillowcases and sheets? Yuki thought, eyeing the pile. Frantically tearing through the packages, she indeed found more pillowcases, a set of sheets, and a satin nightgown. Spotting Kaname's card, Yuki opened it to find another message:

Sweet dreams. —Kaname

Yuki gazed at the bounty around her. *I get the feeling he's not just celebrating my perfect test score anymore...*

In fact she was beginning to suspect that he was using the pretext of celebrating her academic achievements so she would accept his lavish gifts. There was no way he would be this happy she had scored well on her test, right?

"It was just one perfect score...You're spoiling me too much, Kaname-sama."

After she had dressed, Yuki went down to the dining room

and found Seiren there.

"Yuki-sama, may I pour you some tea?"

"Is my brother out again?" Yuki asked as she seated herself at the table. She hadn't sensed his presence in the house since she'd woken. Lately it seemed he was always busy, returning home each day after she'd gone to sleep and leaving again well before she rose. The days had continued to pass in that manner.

It's because the senate is no more, Yuki thought.

During Rido's attack on Cross Academy in pursuit of Yuki, Kaname had been busy destroying the vampire senate. No longer hindered by the senate's oversight, a certain faction of vampires had gone wild and started attacking humans at will again. As a pureblood, Kaname was working to build a new body of governance and was busy with its preparations. Yuki knew that he must have been exhausted, yet he'd managed to bring all those gifts and make over her room without waking her. It was an endearing feat.

It may be because I've always felt protective of him, but...I wish he'd just rest when he's at home.

While Yuki sat lost in thought, a teacup was set before her. It was filled with royal milk tea, prepared with extra milk. Yuki took a sip, savoring the mellow sweetness of the milk and the slight bitter edge of the fragrant tea leaves.

"Seiren, may I ask you something about my brother, Kaname? I'm sure this is an odd question, but he didn't say anything like, 'Pleasant bedding makes for better-quality sleep, thus improving brain functions,' did he?"

"No, I don't remember Kaname-sama saying anything like that."

"O-okay..."

I'm becoming paranoid. Why can't I just happily accept his presents? This isn't how I want to be...

Suddenly feeling fatigued, Yuki gave a soft sigh.

What am I going to do? If I don't get a perfect score on my next test I'll be in trouble. After all, she didn't want to disappoint Kaname. But Yuki felt anything but confident in her own academic ability.

In any case, I've got to get him to stop this gift attack. I can't handle any more pressure than I'm already under!

Before Dawn

Yuki had kept herself awake until Kaname's return and had finally conveyed her concerns to him.

"K-Kaname-sama, there's something I'd like to speak with you about."

"What is it, Yuki? Again with the formality."

"Thank you very much for all the congratulatory gifts. But anything more would be..."

Yuki fought to keep speaking evenly as her face became redder and redder. Watching her, Kaname chuckled softly.

"I understand," he said. "Let this be the last, then."

I knew he was going to bring something tonight too! Yuki thought, her shoulders stiffening. Wondering what in the world it would be this time, she watched Kaname reach into the breast pocket of his coat and withdraw a long flat box topped with a ribbon. Inside, Yuki found an elegant fountain pen. Its slim white body was inlaid with a delicate pattern of sparkling prisms.

"This is..."

"It's an antique fountain pen. I thought it was appropriate since you really seem to be making progress in your studies."

Oof!

Yuki's heart was all but seizing from the pressure.

"Th-thank you very much. I shall treasure it always..."

Managing a strained smile, Yuki politely accepted the fountain pen.

Meanwhile Aido was feeling the pressure as well. To commemorate Yuki's perfect score, he had placed the momentous answer sheet in a frame and hung it on the wall of the study room.

But this giant flower mark drawn all over the paper...

It went without saying that for Aido, the flower mark ignited a certain acute spark of rivalry and displeasure. *Oh, that's just so like Kaname-sama,* he told himself. Aided by the overflowing adoration he had for Kaname in his heart, he made himself accept it with a measure of grace.

However, his subsequent worry was whether this amazing feat could ever be repeated. A chill ran down his spine as he tried to gauge the likelihood.

One miracle followed by yet another? No, there's no way real life ever works out that conveniently, he thought. *And the person in question is Yuki Cross. There's no way she'll be able to achieve two perfect scores in a row!*

Aido glanced over at Yuki, who sat hunched over some chemistry problems.

Absolutely impossible! Her head is already working overtime right now!

Yuki was definitely in one of her signature "I don't even know what I don't understand" poses. To Aido it looked as though the heavy aura surrounding her was increasing exponentially.

There's not much chance she'll get another 100 percent in this state, he thought. Aido could imagine just how disappointed Kaname would be...

Except he wouldn't be disappointed. He would be furious. *And I know just on whom he'll focus the brunt of that fury,* Aido thought, clutching at his head. *There's no mistake—Kaname-sama will definitely come after me, hurling curses in that thundering voice like something calling out from the pits of hell! Even though it's all Yuki Cross's fault for being such a scatterbrain, he'll say it's because my tutoring wasn't good enough and impart all the blame to me!*

Aido couldn't imagine how he would work up the courage to look Kaname directly in the eyes when the time came. There was no other option. No matter what, Yuki had to get another perfect score on the next test. Absolutely.

"Yuki Cross...Yuki Kuran...Eh, I mean, Yuki-sama. Tomorrow I'm going to give you a chemistry test. So please be sure to review your notes very carefully tonight."

"Huh? You're already giving me another test?"

"Don't make that face at me! You just scored a perfect 100 percent on your last one. Just have more confidence in yourself. Your score last time wasn't a fluke. It's proof as to how good you are with your studies now." Aido applauded himself on saying the lie easily.

"Um...But I don't feel confident at all," Yuki muttered, her face downcast. "I didn't even understand half of what we covered today. Getting another perfect score now feels as far off and out of reach as a star shining in the night sky."

Seeing Yuki thoroughly wrapped in her aura of gloom, Aido scowled as he bit down hard on his lip. This girl was a pureblood vampire! How dare she have so little self-confidence? Wasn't keeping a cool, confident exterior no matter what the situation at the very core of a pureblood's dignity? Furthermore, until recent generations, the Kurans had ruled over the vampire realm. Seeing a princess of the royal pureblood clan act like a silly girl was more than Aido could handle.

Come to terms with the elite pureblood you are already!

With great effort, Aido quelled the urge to start scolding her again. She was not only a pureblood vampire princess, but she was also the younger sister of someone he greatly respected.

She is simply used to being Yuki Cross, a hopeless, ordinary schoolgirl from the Day Class who constantly had to stay after school to take extra classes. But that thought gave him an idea.

"That's right, let me give you a little hint for tomorrow. If you study from this section to this section in the textbook, you'll be able to handle any question on the test."

"R-really?"

"Yes! Really!" Aido gave her a firm nod of his head and—struck with a sudden inspiration—clasped her shoulder in a steady, reassuring grip. He gazed earnestly into her eyes and said, "You can do it if you try! I believe in you!"

Next Night

"Did you study hard yesterday?"

"I did! I studied really hard!"

"Good. Then just have confidence in yourself. If you keep calm while you take the test, I know you'll be fine."

"Right!"

"In that case—begin!"

Upon Aido's signal, Yuki flipped over the test paper and got immediately to work on the first problem.

Ah, this is one of the things I reviewed last night! Just as Aido had hinted, she knew exactly how to solve this problem based on the passages she had studied. Even if getting another perfect score was out of reach, Yuki was suddenly hopeful that she could get a good enough score to merit a "you worked hard."

With that thought in mind, Yuki fought to recall as much of what she had studied in the textbook as possible. As a result, she was able to neatly solve the second and third problems, one after the other.

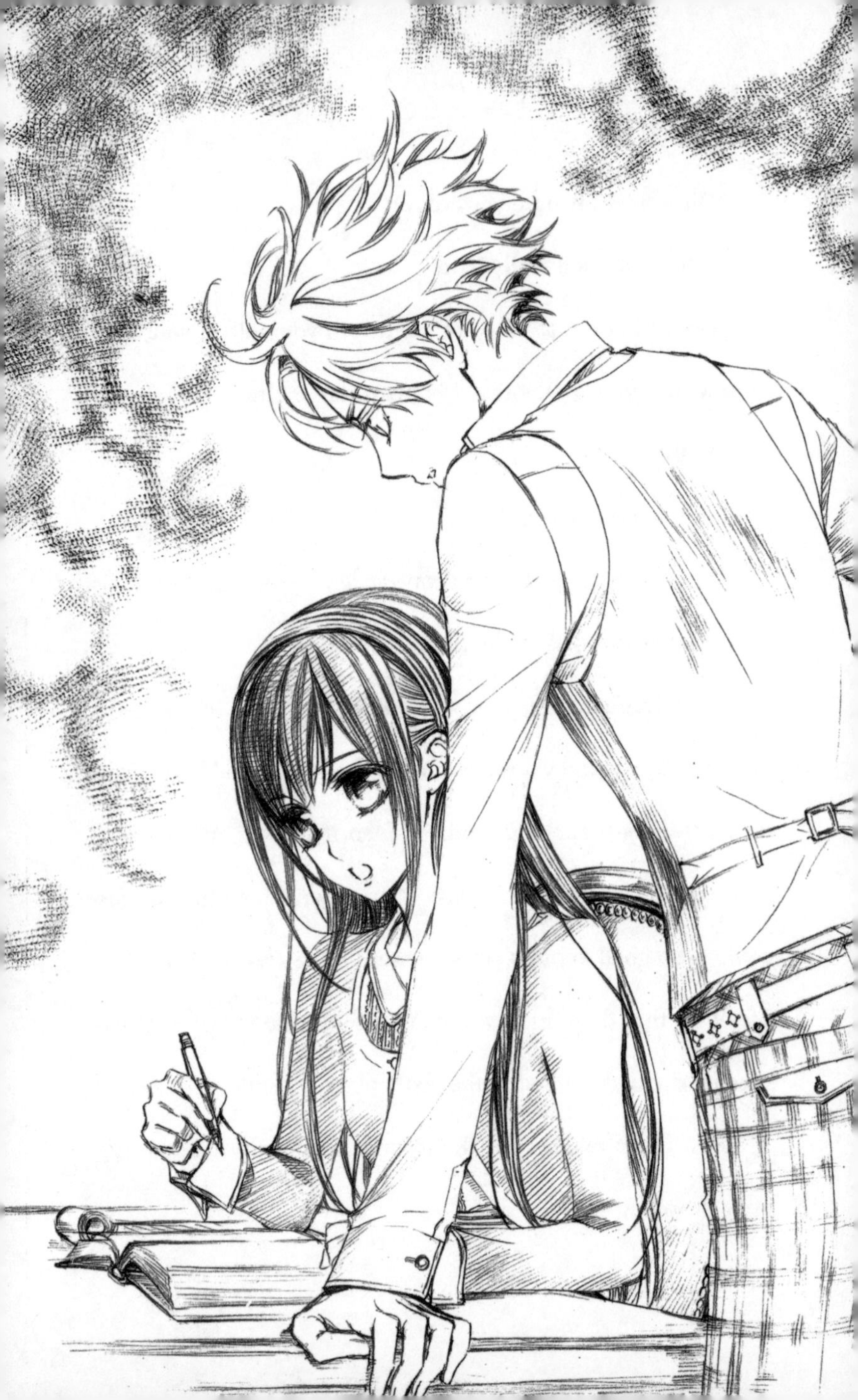

Wow...I can't believe I was able to answer those questions so smoothly and quickly. Despite her earlier trepidation, Yuki found herself turning the test in before the allotted time was up.

I bet this fountain pen had something to do with how I was able to stay so calm and solve all the problems, she thought. As she waited for Aido to grade her test, she gazed down at the sleek, white fountain pen Kaname had presented to her. Perhaps it was a waste to use an antique pen like this to do homework, but she thought of it as a good luck charm for her studies.

At last, she received the anxiously awaited results.

"Another perfect score!"

Aido had scrawled an even larger "100%" on her test than he had the last time.

"I did it...I really did it, Aido!" Yuki could feel herself trembling, barely able to conceive that it had happened twice in a row.

"You sure did. Well done."

"This is all thanks to you. Thank you so much for all

your help!"

"No, you're the one who did the work..." Aido muttered, blushing slightly. Being thanked by her flustered him somehow.

To hide his embarrassment, Aido cleared his throat loudly and said, "This doesn't mean you can let up on your studies. Make sure you review just as hard for all your tests going forward!"

Having returned to her room, Yuki plopped down onto the bed. She raised the answer sheet that she had clutched in both hands toward the ceiling and stared at it.

"Another perfect score..."

Gazing upon the rare sight of a red "100%" on her test results, Yuki finally let herself grin. She had gotten a perfect score twice in a row—and on math and chemistry, no less!

"I guess I really can do it if I put my mind to it," she murmured.

She had worked as a guardian of the school back at Cross Academy. The job had required her to spend her nights patrolling the campus. It had been her duty to deal with Day Class students who snuck out of the Sun Dorm at night and wandered around in hopes of meeting students in the Night Class. As a result she had typically returned to her own dorm around daybreak to catch a few, all-too-brief hours of sleep. She then went about her day severely sleep-deprived. She was always sleepy in class and spent most of the lesson battling sleep rather than actually focusing on what the teacher was saying.

Considering my situation back then, no wonder I could never concentrate in class, she thought. Yuki knew her work as a guardian had been vital, but she still felt a bit of regret that she had wound up neglecting her studies so badly as a result.

I used to fall asleep in class pretty frequently. Yori was always nudging me awake.

Whenever Yuki had lost her ongoing battle against sleep in class, it had often fallen on her roommate and best friend,

Sayori Wakaba, to wake her up. "You shouldn't push yourself so hard, Yuki," she would say. For Yuki, having someone who watched out for her and cared about her was enough to keep her happily doing her job.

"I wonder how Yori is doing now..." Yuki hadn't been able to see her since the day Rido had attacked the academy. *I wish I could see her again.*

Tears welled up in Yuki's eyes before she realized it. It was always like this when she thought of her best friend. Though she knew it was pointless to cry about it, she could feel her spirits flagging.

There's no point in crying. Crying isn't going to change anything at all, she told herself sternly and rolled onto her side.

"Right now, I just need to focus on doing what I can do. I've got to take my studies seriously and find a way to be of more help to Kaname."

Even Aido was working his hardest overseeing Yuki's education. She had to find a way to acknowledge his efforts as well. Thinking hard on the matter, Yuki suddenly had an idea.

"That's it—I should do something for him to express my thanks!"

Though trying to figure out what the something should be was easier said than done.

*That's right, I can't leave the house yet...*She could ask Seiren to go out and buy something for her.

But asking someone else to go buy a gift to express my gratitude is kind of weird, she thought. What good is a gift if you don't take the time and effort to pick it out yourself?

"Hmm, what should I do?"

As she pondered, Yuki caught sight of the flowers around her room.

"That reminds me...Aido likes his bed linens to smell like lavender," Yuki said to herself, suddenly recalling the conversation. Back at Cross Academy, Aido had once decided to run away from the Moon Dorm and wound up spending the night at Headmaster Cross's private residence. Yuki remembered how Aido—despite all his complaints and fussing—had wound up eating substantial quantities of the food Zero made for him. Among the many requirements Aido had for spending the night was sleeping on linens that smelled of lavender.

"Zero looked so annoyed that night," Yuki recalled with a mischievous chuckle, picturing Zero's scowl and the way he had mumbled, "It's fine. I don't hate cooking," as he demonstrated his culinary skills.

"What great memories...Those were such fun times."

Zero...

He was both vampire and vampire hunter. And now he was her enemy as well. They would never again be able to live happily beneath the same roof. The thought made Yuki's chest tighten. She quickly closed her eyes and willed the pain to pass.

Thoughts of Zero raised all sorts of complicated feelings in her. Like the tiny ripples the wind stirred on the surface of water, thinking about Zero stirred up troubling emotions in her heart.

No, no, no! Right now, I'm thinking about what gift to get Aido to thank him! Yuki pushed her unsettled feelings into the back of her mind and forced herself to shift mental gears to the task at hand.

"Here we go!" Yuki said, approaching the bounty of flowers. She went to work searching for any sign of lavender but came up empty-handed. "No lavender flowers anywhere..." Her shoulders slumped in disappointment, but she reminded herself this was no time to give up.

"Hmm..." She gazed at the flowers as she thought. "I've got it!" And with that Yuki hurried off to the library.

"Yes! Here it is!"

Having found the book she was looking for, Yuki quickly flipped it open and skimmed through it until she found the section she wanted. The flowers in her room were so fragrant that Yuki had decided to try making an excellent potpourri or aromatherapy oil from them.

"But wow, there are so many different methods to extract

aromatherapy oil," she murmured. She read further. To extract the essential oil from flowers for aromatherapy, one could use distillation, a pressure-cooking method, or even solvents. "This almost seems like a chemistry experiment."

As she read over the steps each method entailed, Yuki felt her head begin to droop.

No! she scolded herself. *If I can't even do this, I'm useless!*

"In short..."

She opened the notebook she had brought with her and began writing the steps out in simple bullet points to get the ideas clear in her head.

- *Method of choice: Distillation*
- *Put the raw flowers into the distillation chamber and let hot steam pass through it from below*
- *Cool the steam (now containing the scented oil) using a cooling tube, allowing it to turn back into a mixture of water and oil and collect in a beaker*
- *Separate the oil from the water and what's left is essential oil!*

"Okay, I've got it now..."

Now I've just got to do it! Yuki clenched her fist determinedly and nodded firmly to herself.

"But since I'm taking the trouble to make this oil for Aido, it'd be nice to use a fragrance that would suit him." Thinking that, Yuki was suddenly struck by another possibly reckless idea. She would make Aido a custom-scented oil.

Double-checking what materials she would need for her plan, Yuki quickly sprang into action, heading first to find Seiren.

"I was hoping to use a few things today. Do we have anything like this in the house?" Yuki asked her.

"Is this for some manner of experiment?"

"Y-yes, a chemistry experiment. Um, if we don't have these things, I'm sorry to ask, but could you go out and buy them for me?"

"We have them."

"We do?!"

"Please wait one moment. I shall gather them for you immediately."

"Oh—wait a sec! Before you do that..."

Seiren waited patiently.

"If possible, I'd like to have this all set up someplace other than my study room. A room that would be appropriate for doing experiments."

Seiren paused to consider it for a moment, then nodded. "In that case, please follow me."

She led Yuki to a currently unused guest parlor in a corner of the large house.

"This room has a good-sized table that you can make use of, and it shouldn't be a problem if you end up making a bit of a mess, I believe. Will this room do?"

"Absolutely! Thank you, Seiren! You're a lifesaver!"

"I shall call you once all the materials you requested have been gathered." With that, Seiren turned on her heel to go. Yuki called her back quickly.

"Um, Seiren, can you also make sure no one comes into this room? I want to keep this a secret from both my brother and Aido."

Seiren hesitated for just a moment before replying, "Of course, Yuki-sama," her expression never changing. She bowed and was gone in an instant.

She's like a ninja, Yuki thought.

"Okay, then—first things first!" Yuki returned to her room and began clearing off her tabletop.

"Neigh!"

Astride a white horse, Yuki was galloping around the horse yard at Cross Academy. The horse in question was the famously wild-spirited White Lily, and Yuki could hardly believe that she was able to ride her.

I mean, it's White Lily! I'm really riding her!

Yuki couldn't help letting out a whoop and laughing.

Behind the fence surrounding the horse yard stood Sayori, who was watching and waving at her.

"Yuki! This is amazing! You're a genius!"

When Yuki looked over at her, she found that Zero and Kageyama, the Day Class representative, were also there. Soon Ichijo, Kain, Ruka, Rima, Shiki, and the rest of the Night Class were cheering her on, exclaiming things like, "Brilliant! As expected!"

Heh. It looks like I'm finally being acknowledged by everyone.

When Yuki's ride finally ended and she dismounted White Lily, she turned and gave her beautiful coat a tender pat.

"Thank you, White Lily," she said, holding a carrot out toward the horse's mouth in thanks. However, Lily ignored the carrot and chomped down on Yuki's head instead.

"No! That's my head!" Yuki was yelling when she suddenly noticed an aroma wafting faintly from her body.

Huh?

She looked down and saw that she was dressed in a full-body carrot costume.

"I-I'm some sort of carrot girl?!"

"Neigh!"

"No, wait! I'm not a carrot!" Yuki cried, running in terror as Lily galloped crazily after her. Yuki could see White Lily's eyes were those of a hunter chasing down its prey!

"No! No! Someone save me!"

"Hey, wake up!" At the sound of Aido's voice and the vigorous shake on her shoulder, Yuki raised her groggy eyes from the desk she had been sprawled over.

"Mm? Aido? I'm not a carrot, you know...? I wouldn't...be tasty...if you bit me..."

"Huh? What the heck are you saying?! Do you think I would want to bite you? Don't be so full of yourself just because you managed to get two perfect test scores in a row on my tests!"

Aido was thoroughly offended that Yuki had nodded off in his class.

"Sorry," Yuki apologized sheepishly. Aido sighed.

"Did you not get enough sleep last night? You've got bags under your eyes. I can see them. What were you doing up so late?"

"I-I was studying of course! I've got to work hard for the next test too!"

"Hmmm." Aido narrowed his eyes in suspicion.

"H-honest, I was! Especially chemistry. I really understand it now!"

"Really?"

"Yes, really!"

"Okay, then. I look forward to your next test result." Aido still didn't look convinced, but dropped the matter. He opened the textbook instead. "Now, read the section you missed while you were dozing off."

"R-right!"

Alert again, Yuki turned quickly to her textbook.

Sorry, Aido, she apologized silently. *I can't tell you the truth just yet!*

Around that time, in the entrance hall of the great house...

Clad in a long black coat, Kaname stood near the door while Seiren waited attentively nearby.

"I'll be on my way then," he said.

As Seiren bowed to him, he suddenly paused and glanced back over his shoulder.

"That reminds me," he said. "It seems Yuki hasn't been sleeping well lately?"

"She is quite busy with her chemistry experiments."

"Experiments? Hmm...I suppose it's part of her studies?"

"It appears so."

"I see. She must have gained some self-confidence after the improvement in her test scores. Well, it's never a bad thing to be interested in a variety of things. But do tell her that she's not allowed to overtire herself."

"Yes, Kaname-sama."

"Oh, and one more thing..." Kaname pulled two envelopes from the inner pocket of his coat and handed them to Seiren. They were invitations to the upcoming soirée they were hosting. "I'd like you to deliver these to Shirabuki Manor."

"Both of them, Kaname-sama?"

"Yes. Thank you."

Seiren glanced down at the envelopes. In addition to the one for Sara, the other was addressed to Takuma Ichijo.

"I'll be off then." With a toss of his long coat, Kaname turned and stepped into the night, melding into its darkness.

A few days later...

"*Fuaaah.*" Yuki gave an enormous yawn as she stepped into the study.

"Yuki Cross! Honestly, how rude!" Aido immediately scolded her.

"Sorry about that, Aido."

"Did you not get enough sleep again? I'm glad you love studying now, but you can't let it wreck your health. What have you got if you don't have your health?"

"Right..." she mumbled, her shoulders drooping at having been scolded. But Yuki immediately perked back up. "A-actually, Aido! Before we start class, there's something I wanted to give you. Here, it's a little thank-you gift for everything you've done for me lately."

She held out to him a small gift box wrapped with a light blue ribbon.

"For me? A gift?"

"Yes! Please go ahead and open it."

"O-okay...Sure." Looking a bit red about the ears, Aido opened the box and found inside a small glass bottle and what appeared to be a decorative cushion, roughly the size of his palm.

"What is this?" he asked, poking the cushion lightly. Its contents made a rustling noise.

"It's a scent sachet. There's potpourri inside," Yuki explained. "It has a nice scent, don't you think?"

Aido raised the sachet to his nose and sniffed. It had a sweet, light, floral fragrance.

"Um...what do you think?" Yuki asked.

"It definitely does smell nice," said Aido. "But what's with the quality of this thing?" The seams holding the sachet together were large and sloppy, and the tiny ribbon attached to it was off-center. Aido almost wanted to ask if a little kid had made it, but he managed to contain himself.

"I made it myself," Yuki confessed. "I made the potpourri inside of it too. And the aromatherapy oil in the bottle."

"What?!" Aido exclaimed. "You seriously made all of this yourself?"

"Yeah. By the way, the scent of the aromatherapy oil is my own original blend. I tried to come up with a custom scent for you based on your personality."

"A custom scent for me, huh..." Aido repeated. "That's

rather amazing!" He plucked the bottle from its box and popped off the lid. Immediately, a sweet scent rose out of it, tickling Aido's nose.

It smells really nice. It pains me to say it, but she did a good job matching a scent for me. I think I really like it.

"Wait a minute," Aido said, "don't tell me this is what you've been up to that's made you lose all that sleep lately?"

"Um, yes," Yuki said. "I wanted it to be a surprise, so I had to keep it a secret from you." Yuki lowered her face, letting her hair fall forward to hide a sheepish grin. "But I really had fun making the aromatherapy oil. It felt like I was doing a chemistry experiment. I had lots of failures in the beginning, but I kept trying it over and over. When I finally got the scent just right, I was so happy! Feeling a sense of accomplishment is a great thing, isn't it?"

To think she'd go and try an experiment like that on her own... She's really progressed, hasn't she? Aido thought. Considering how crazily he'd worked to try to tutor her these past months, he couldn't help but feel extremely pleased and simply stood there, not realizing he'd fallen silent.

"Um, so, you can put the sachet in a desk or closet or wherever you like," Yuki continued.

"Yes. I'll do that." As he was wondering to himself where he would put it, Aido reached over to pick up the sachet and smell it one more time. However, it suddenly gave way in his hand. A cascade of dried flower petals fluttered to the floor.

"Huh?"

Looking closely, Aido realized that one of the loose stitches was so wide that there was a sizeable hole in one corner of the sachet.

"I'm so sorry!" Yuki cried. "I'm really terrible at sewing. Please give it back. I'll fix it right now!" She reached up to pull the sachet out of Aido's hands.

"Hold on a second! You don't have to do it right now!" Aido was saying, when he caught his foot on the leg of the desk and stumbled.

"Ah!"

"Aido?!" Yuki reached out to grab him before he fell but tripped on the rug and lost her balance as well.

"Watch it!"

Thud!

"Be more careful, you—" Aido fell silent. All the blood drained from his face. Somehow he had wound up landing on top of Yuki in such a way that it would appear he was pinning her down.

Worse yet, Yuki had been knocked unconscious beneath him.

If a particular someone were to see us now, I would be dead, Aido thought.

"Hey! Wake up, already! Come on!" he cried, shaking Yuki's shoulder desperately.

At that moment, Aido heard the creak of the study door slowly swinging open. A terrible sense of misgiving swept over him.

"What do you think you're doing to Yuki, Aido?"

Oh no!

The dark, heavy voice that seemed to reverberate from the depths of hell was in the room with him. Aido trembled. Kaname's crimson eyes stared down darkly.

"K-Kaname-sama!"

"Did you push Yuki down?"

"W-welcome home, Kaname-sama! This isn't...Um, it's not what it looks like—"

"And just what does it look like? You dare say that to me right now?"

But the unfortunate scene wasn't the only thing bothering Kaname.

"I've been aware for some time that Yuki has been losing sleep to conduct experiments. I also knew it was in order to make a surprise present for someone. But to think that some-one was you, Aido..."

There was not a trace of good humor in Kaname's eyes.

Aido shrank farther back, all the while knowing he had no possible hope of escape.

"B-but it was a surprise! I had no idea what she was up to!" he cried desperately, but Kaname's slow, ominous approach did not cease.

"Even so," said Kaname, "there is something else that's been bothering me, Aido. You went easy on Yuki for that second test, didn't you? You wanted to appease both her and myself, so you set the test up in a way that would make it easy for her to get full marks again. Do you think a tutor rigging a test is acceptable?"

"W-well, I..."

He knows! Aido was frantic.

"You have such excellent instincts, Aido. I'm sure you know what I will do next."

He gave Aido a chilling smile, and then...

"Aaaaaaah!"

Aido's anguished wails echoed repeatedly through the walls

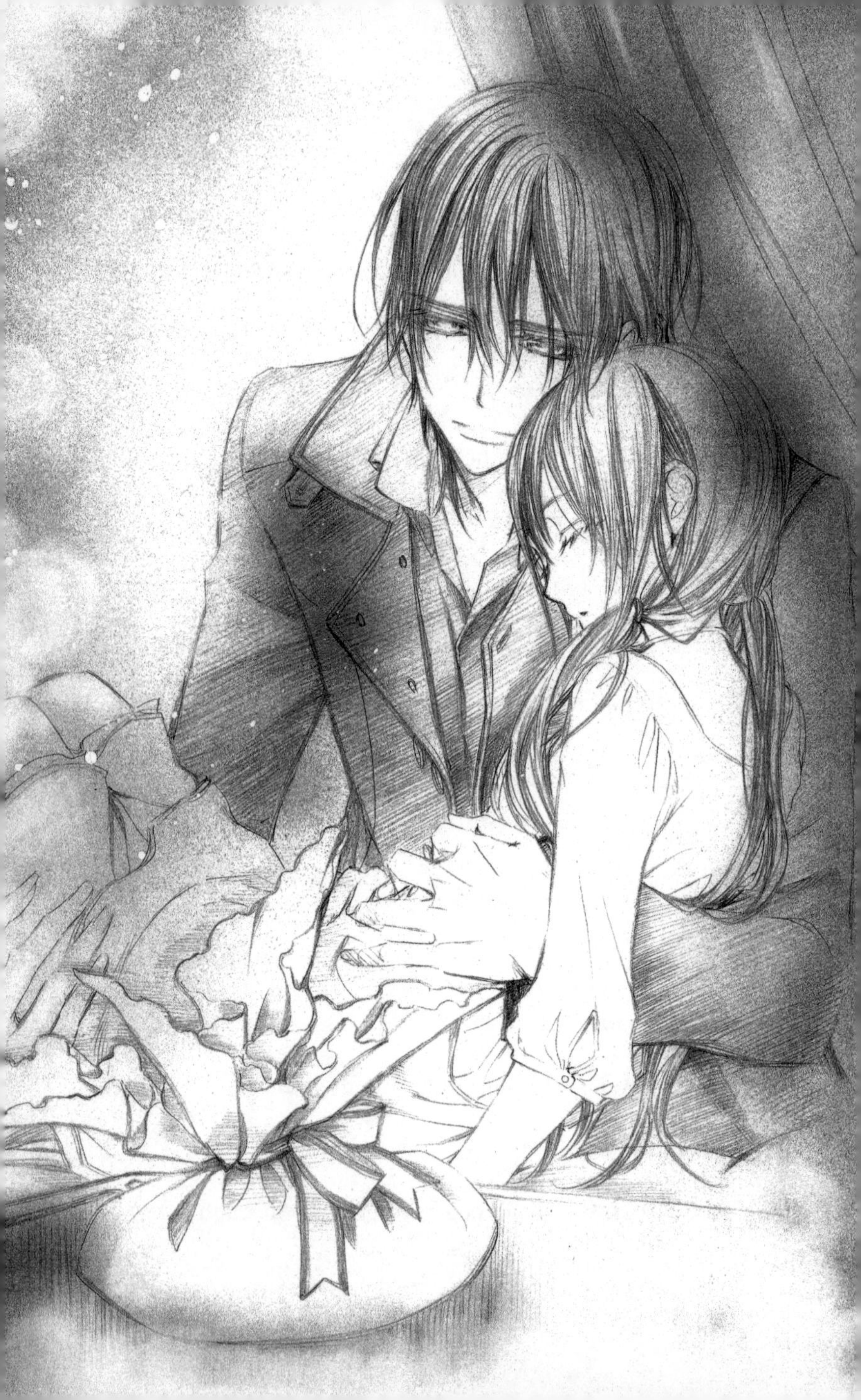

of the study room.

"Why do I keep finding you sleeping in such places?" Kaname asked, kneeling on the floor beside the slumbering Yuki. Slipping his arms beneath her slender form, he picked her gently up in his arms.

Yuki didn't stir at all. She continued slumbering with a contented look on her face. After so many days without adequate sleep, her body had taken its chance to continue resting after she'd collapsed. Kaname carried her up to her room and laid her carefully on her bed.

"You are a troublesome girl, aren't you? Though that's just another thing I love about you." He silently brushed back a few strands of hair that had fallen against her cheek when something on her side table caught his eye.

"What's this?"

It appeared to be another present.

I see...So she made one for me too, Kaname thought. She had likely meant to give it to him the following night, since he had already left the house before she'd awoke.

Leaving the gift where it was, Kaname laid a gentle kiss on Yuki's cheek.

"I'll look forward to tomorrow, then," he said. "Good night, Yuki."

He went out of the room, closing the door quietly behind him. In her bed, Yuki turned over and slept on peacefully.

HIDDEN
LOVE

The first time I met him was on a night with a hazy moon.

On that night…

There had been a discreet gaiety throughout the manor that night. Rather than a grand ball, Father had thrown a simple dinner party. I remember hearing the murmuring speech and quiet laughter of the adults. Music played softly in the background, so as not to disrupt their conversation. I remember the women in beautiful gowns that gave color and brightness to the night.

But I had turned my back to all that, and I was sitting and

crying quietly in the garden. I didn't want to cry, but the tears wouldn't stop. I hated myself for that, which only made me cry all the more.

As I sat there sobbing, I heard a soft voice.

"Sara-sama? What is the matter?"

I looked up at the source of that soft voice only after I'd wiped my eyes vigorously. As a pureblood I couldn't afford to show my teary face to anyone no matter what the circumstances.

A young man stood before me, gazing at me with worried eyes. Over his shoulder, blurred through my tears, I saw a hazy moon in the night sky.

"Nothing is the matter," I replied.

"Then why were you crying?" he asked. The man was a stranger to me. And yet something about him made my fettered heart come undone. I wound up telling him the truth.

"I've lost my hairpin," I told him between sobs. "I really... liked it so. But I...can't find it...anywhere!"

"Is that so? Now, that is a problem, isn't it?"

He listened to my childish woes and answered me seriously, without even a hint of a smile. He knelt down on one knee before me and, gazing up at me, said, "In that case, Sara-sama, allow me to cast a magic spell that will bring back your smile!"

He snapped his fingers and shaped them to look like a bird. He twirled his fingers and a rose appeared in his hands. He offered it to me.

"Oh my…"

It was a rose of a dark red color, as though it had drunk in the dark of the night. But the moment I reached out to take the rose, a single petal immediately fluttered down from the blossom. Then suddenly, as if disturbed by a brief wind in the night, all the petals showered down onto the ground.

Just now—was that this man's "power"?

He wasn't trying to give me a rose? Why would he make the petals fall? I wondered that as I stared into his eyes.

"Sara-sama, as vampires our lives stretch onward to eternity, yet everything else of this world is fleeting. But perhaps it is due to the very nature of these fleeting things that in their one brief moment, they shine so very brightly."

"…"

Without realizing it, I had opened my eyes wide. For the words he had spun upon his honeyed lips found their way into my heart and had become my brief, shining moment.

As I stood there watching him in a daze, he said, "If your heart shone with joy in the brief moment you wore your hairpin, isn't that enough?"

He reached over to a nearby rosebush and, selecting the single, most beautiful white rose from the lot, plucked it from its stem. The pale orange color that warmed the depths of its center appeared to me like a candle in the night's darkness. I felt jealous of this rose that he had plucked with his fingers.

"I beg your pardon."

He drew so close to me that I could feel his breath on my cheek. My shoulders stiffened as I felt the barest touch of his fingers against my hair.

He drew back a little, and I watched his lips murmur, "To the shine of a single moment."

He had tucked the rose into my hair like a hairpin.

"It suits you," he said, and smiled.

Not long after that night I entered our scheduled hibernation along with my parents.

Asato Ichijo-sama...

That was his name.

That night I had gained two things: his name and the faint kindling of new feeling that glowed in my heart...

I wonder if he'll ever come to see me again. Dreaming of our reunion, I let my eyes slide shut.

A very long time passed while I was locked in that cold, frozen space.

I slept a long, dreamless sleep. And when I woke, the memory of him was still there, sure and clear inside me.

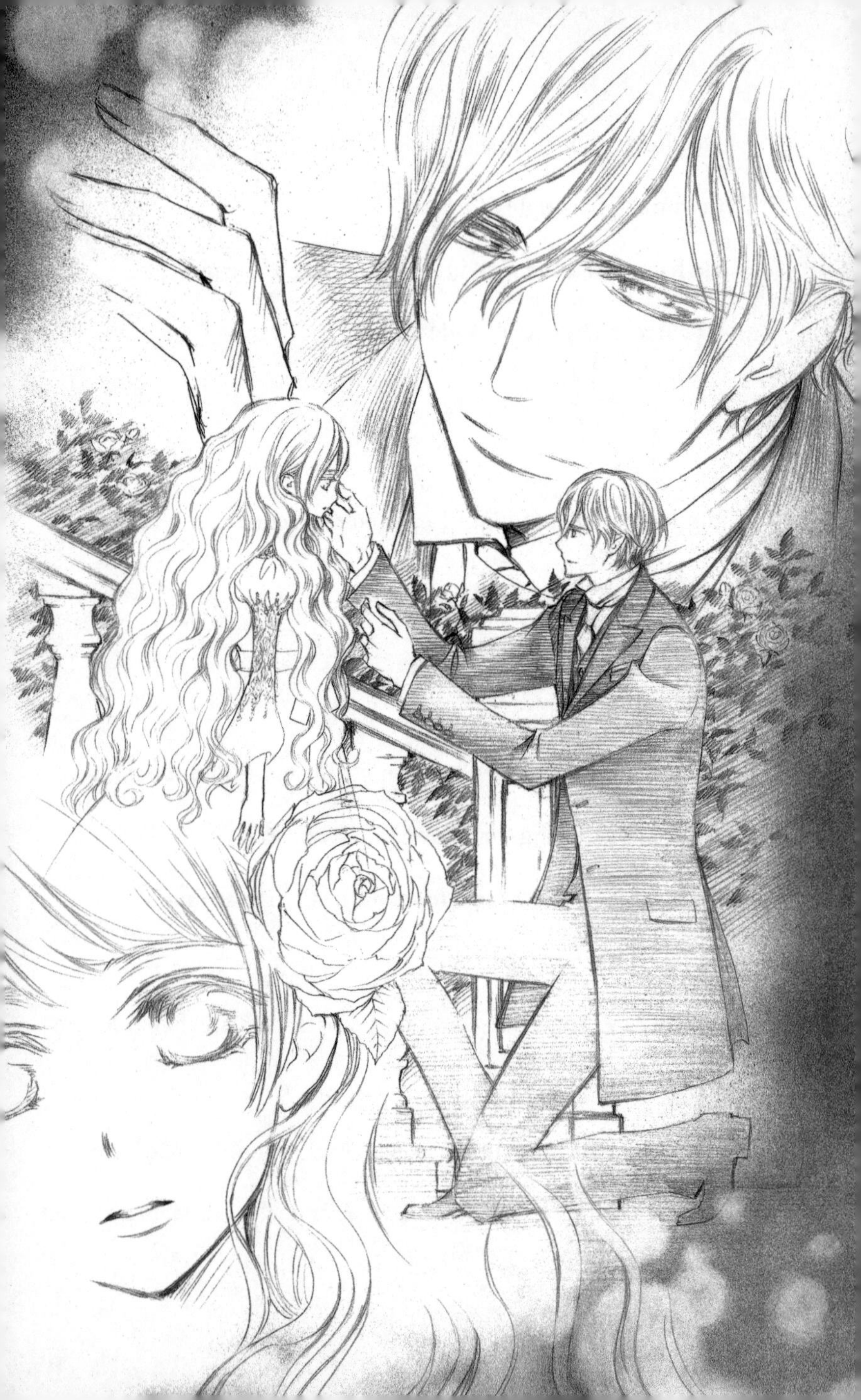

The moment it arose in me, I gasped aloud.

Retracing the memory, I stepped out into the garden. Amid all the roses blooming gloriously, I sought one that looked like the rose he had picked for me that night—petals in the color of soft white silk and a center hued in shades of the setting sun.

This one.

We would soon hold a ball here. Perhaps he would come again. Thinking of that, I had something specially prepared for that night.

On the night of the ball, I was escorted into the ballroom by Ouri-sama.

"Sara-sama!"

"Oh, she's the one."

"How lovely!"

Everyone had their eyes on me. *But it isn't their eyes that I want staring at me*, I thought. And it certainly wasn't

Ouri-sama's amber gaze either.

What I wished for...What I truly wanted was...

Entering the ballroom, my attention was caught and held by a dignified older gentleman. But why? An odd feeling filled my chest. I asked Ouri-sama, "Who is that gentleman?"

"Oh, that's Ichio. That is, Lord Asato Ichijo."

"Ichio..."

The flow of time is cruel. During the long years I'd slept, he had grown old. I, on the other hand, still had the form of a young girl, unchanged from that day. The gap between us felt insurmountable. Even though Ouri-sama was right beside me, and so many other people in the room were there with me, I suddenly felt inconsolably alone.

"He's the leader of the old generation," Ouri-sama was saying. "In the human world, he heads the Ichijo Group as its chief executive. Humans fear and respect him..."

"I see."

He noticed my eyes on him. Ichio held my gaze from across

the room as he made his way toward me.

"Ouri-sama, Sara-sama, it has been too long."

"Lord Asato! No, we must learn to call you 'Ichio' as well, mustn't we?"

"As it pleases you."

As Ichio made a small bow to us, he reached beside him and gently pushed a small boy forward.

"May I present my grandson Takuma?"

"My name is Takuma Ichijo. It is a great honor to make your acquaintances, Ouri-sama, Sara-sama," said the little boy. He looked at me and gave me a shy smile.

After we'd made our introductions I excused myself from Ouri-sama, telling him I wished to take in the night air alone. As I stepped out onto the balcony, the wind passing through the darkness of the night sky played softly through my hair. I gently unclipped my hairpin.

It seems he doesn't remember anything about that night.

It had been many long years since I had felt the night wind

in my hair. His face had changed a great deal as well.

I can't believe he introduced his grandson to me.

But what hurt even more was that when he had looked at my hairpin, his face showed no reaction at all.

Ouri-sama was my fiancé. This fate had been decided for us since birth. For purebloods, marrying to preserve the family bloodline was our duty. But surely it was fine at least to dream about love, wasn't it?

I knew that any dream of mine would someday come to an end. But now faced with that certainty, I found my heart was more delicate than I'd expected. My heart was as fragile and brittle as glass.

Looking down at the rose-shaped hairpin in my hand, I began to feel it was a burden to me. I turned toward the garden and threw it as far as I could.

"..."

I was throwing away the past. I no longer needed it. So there was really no reason to be sad.

But my traitorous heart forced my tears to fall once again.

No, I mustn't cry. I'm a proud pureblood vampire!

Just as I was telling myself to get a handle on my emotions, I heard a voice behind me.

"Sara-sama, here..."

Small hands extended themselves toward me. They were holding my rose hairpin.

But I just threw that away...!

I stared at it and said nothing.

"Um...I think you dropped this?" Takuma asked timidly, peeking up at me.

Such an innocent little face. Yet something about it resembled that man.

Yes, it was the eyes. Those eyes that gazed at me. They told me beyond the shadow of a doubt that this boy shared that man's blood.

"..."

I turned away, not wanting to see Takuma's face anymore.

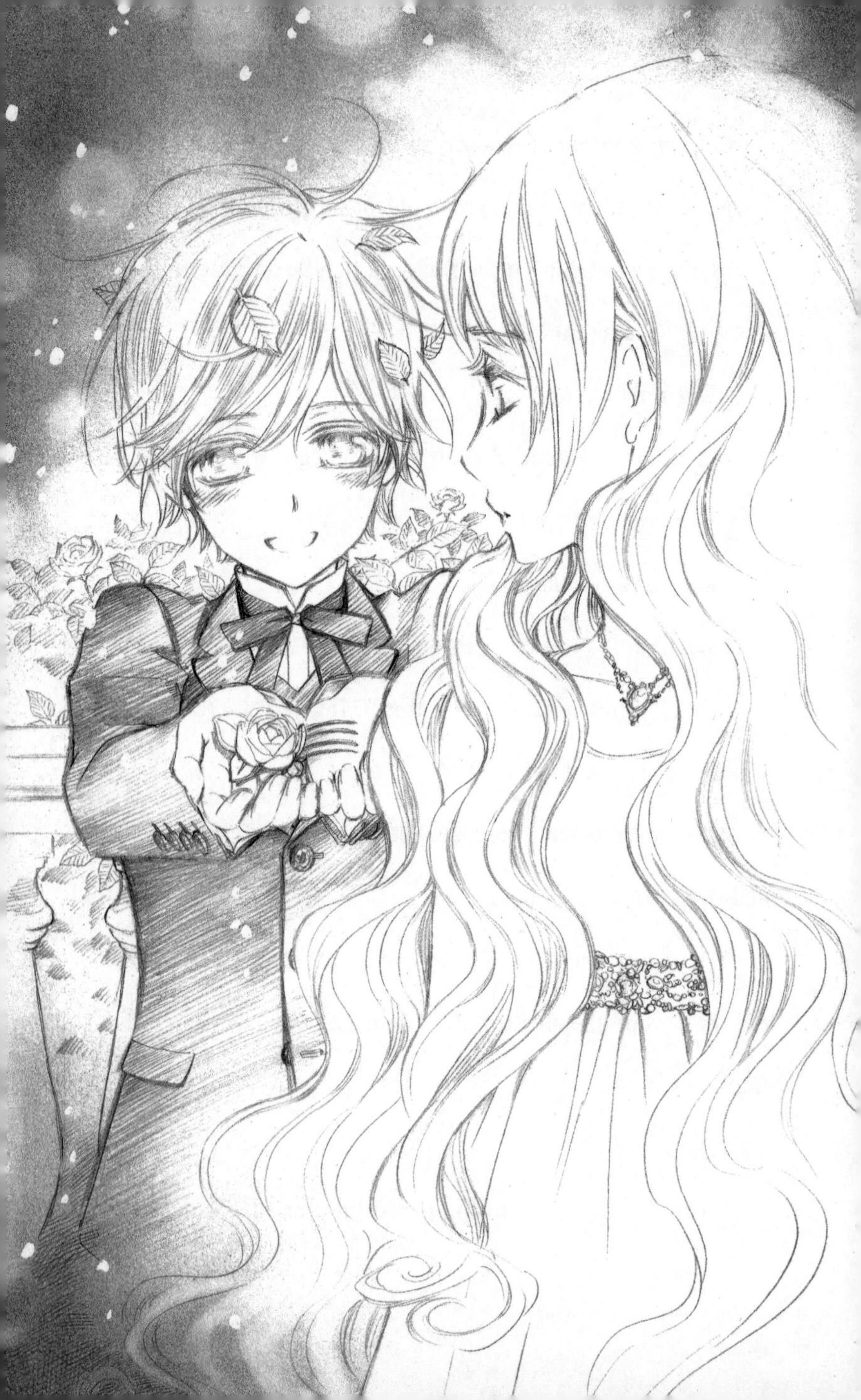

Please, please go away somewhere. Please don't look at me with those eyes. And yet...

"Um...I beg your pardon," he said. His little hands reached up and lightly brushed my hair.

He had placed the hairpin in my hair.

"That's a very pretty hairpin. It suits you very well, Sara-sama," he said, smiling brightly up at me. It reminded me sharply of his grandfather's smile on that night long ago.

Don't sully my beautiful memories!

As my heart grew heavier, I began to lose my patience.

I pulled the hairpin from my hair and threw it as far as I could again.

"Huh? Uh...ah!" Takuma gaped at me and then quickly scurried down to the garden again.

"Can't he understand I'm throwing it away? So why would he..." It was obvious I didn't want it. So why did he feel compelled to retrieve it for me? Takuma's innocent heart irritated me.

The garden was dark with night. And in it I caught sight of a small back searching for a white rose-shaped pin by the light of the moon.

As I watched him, I felt a certain warmth filling my heart.

"That commotion...You didn't do something you shouldn't have, did you?"

It was right as we left the soirée that Kaname was holding at the Kuran residence...

Takuma had asked me that after our car had pulled away, a note of accusation in his mild voice. The little boy of that memory was now a young man—the young man who stayed at my side. His eyes that so resembled those of his grandfather gazed steadily at me as he put his defiant question to me.

"Be quiet."

Unable to conceal my inner irritation, I dug my nails into the car window.

Crack!

Five cracks following the shape of my hand pierced the glass. A faint cool breeze blew in from the fissures.

"Sara?! What did you do?!"

I looked into Takuma's surprised face and confessed.

"I devoured Ouri-sama's life."

It was for that purpose I'd taken control of one of the vampire hunters that had come to patrol the event. I wanted to use her weapon, which could negate the regenerative powers of a pureblood.

Ouri-sama had grown weary of eternal life a long time ago. He did nothing but idly wait for his final moment to arrive.

I don't want to end up like Ouri-sama.

And that man—Ichio—had been lost along with the senate he had controlled. My parents too had perished by my own hand long ago...

In short, there was not a single person left with whom I shared a bond.

"I'm going to become queen."

The slight breeze slipping through the cracks in the window fluttered through my hair.

"You think Kaname will allow that?" Takuma asked, watching me with troubled eyes. I wondered if he was worried for Kaname. Or perhaps for me?

Perhaps that kindness of his was what he'd inherited from the man who had captured my heart.

I narrowed my eyes against the cold breeze. At that time I already knew where my cruel fate would lead me. I'd end up nowhere else but in the deepest darkness at the very edge of the night.

QUEEN
OF THE
ABYSS

Plip. A drop of water fell down into the bathtub. In the middle of a stylish bathroom the tub was filled to the brim with an ominously red liquid. A certain nauseating odor filled the room while an alluringly beautiful woman luxuriated in the bath, stretching her long, supple limbs. The brilliant crimson liquid slid starkly over her porcelain-like white skin. With a lavish flick of her tongue, she lapped up a long trail of the ruby-red blood from the back of her hand.

The woman's mismatched eyes gleamed red and purple like liquid gemstones. She had the kind of volatile intensity that could flare up to immolate anyone who dared stoke it carelessly, and her depraved yet immaculate beauty worked in perfect harmony with this propensity.

Crouching before her was a male subordinate, his head respectfully lowered. On the back of his hand was a curious tattoo depicting red rose petals.

"A few days ago," he reported, "at a soirée hosted by the pureblood Kaname Kuran, another pureblood—a guest named Ouri—committed suicide."

"Oh, really?" said the woman. "Ouri ended his life…"

The warm blood splashed softly as she shifted in the tub. She often had her subordinates report to her as she frolicked about in a bath of blood like this—it alleviated the boredom of it all. But this news actually piqued her interest.

"Even if he had grown weary of the world after his long life, I can't imagine he would have waited to take it while at a soirée with so many attending," she mused.

A pureblood committing suicide…It was the first time she'd ever heard of such a thing. Even though it had been said at the time that Kaname Kuran's parents had killed themselves, everyone now believed that it was really Kaname's uncle Rido who had driven them to their deaths. That incident, which had occurred over ten years ago, seemed to have been the impetus for Rido's recent activities. However, those activities had resulted in Rido's demise at the hands of Kaname's sister while Kaname was busy exterminating every last vampire on the corrupt senate.

Thinking on these events, she let her eyes narrow ruminatively.

"The world of the aristocrats has been in quite an uproar lately, hasn't it?" she said aloud. "Are they quite sure it was suicide?"

"Not yet, Mistress," her servant answered. "It appears it was not a simple suicide. Rumor has it that there was another pureblood behind the deed."

But there had been only a handful of purebloods at the soirée: the host, Kaname Kuran; his younger sister, Yuki; and just one other: Sara Shirabuki, Ouri's fiancée.

"Though if I recall," said the woman, "she's the sort of snooty little rich girl who acts as though she wouldn't hurt a fly. So, what else then? What other juicy tidbits did you uncover for me?"

The look she fixed her subordinate with said there had better be more or he would regret it. The poor man hurriedly continued on with his report.

"It appears that Sara Shirabuki has been keeping Ichio's grandson with her."

"Ichio's? You mean the Ichio who was the leader of the now-defunct senate? She has his grandson?"

"So it would seem."

"What is this grandson's name?"

"Takuma Ichijo, Mistress."

"So the Shirabuki clan and the Ichijo clan together...Hmm. That actually sounds quite interesting. All this just when I was starting to get bored!"

The smile she flashed him was so brilliant that the servant had to lower his eyes because he was unable to meet hers.

"Mistress..." The young man kneeling beside her bathtub moved to extend his bare neck to her, offering his blood of his own will. He murmured her name, gazing at her in an enchanted daze. She glanced over at him, her odd, mismatched eyes glinting with anticipation, and gave him a bedazzling smile.

"Be good and wait for me here, dear boy. I need to go out and have a bit of fun."

She raised her slender fingers to the man's exposed, vulnerable neck and dragged his head toward her. Then, without a moment's hesitation, she bared her fangs and sank her teeth in.

Night. The sound of several sets of running feet echoed across the cobblestone streets of the town. A man was running for his life. A faint scent of blood wafted from him as he gasped for breath, and in his open mouth were a pair of blood-drenched fangs.

"Kaito! He's heading your way!"

"You don't have to tell me that!"

Kaito stood waiting in the alley, his coat billowing out behind him. He cocked his gun.

Realizing he'd fallen into their trap, the fleeing vampire stopped and dropped to his knees.

"P-please...don't kill me," he pleaded, looking beseeching-ly up at Kaito. His victim's blood was still smeared around his mouth.

"That's not open to discussion," Kaito said coldly, pulling the trigger without a hint of emotion in his steady gaze.

The vampire's body, riddled with bullets, tumbled to the ground. Kaito tilted his head to one side.

"That's another one off the list," he said aloud.

The vampire's body slowly turned to ash. Kaito watched the remains being blown across the cobblestones on the night breeze. It was a sight Kaito particularly hated, no matter how many times he had seen it.

"You finished him off?" came a voice over his shoulder.

"Yeah," Kaito confirmed. "But seriously—it's just one after the next. This never seems to end!" He glanced over his shoulder at the newly arrived Zero and heaved a deep sigh. "Now that the senate is gone, we've been getting tons of rampaging vampires around here. They've been keeping us too damn busy."

"And this pus that keeps seeping out of the vampire realm shows no sign of stopping," Zero said grimly.

With the fall of the senate and its role as mitigator of the threat vampires posed to the human world now gone, the number of attacks by rogue vampires was higher than ever. As a result vampire hunters like Zero and Kaito were working to the point of exhaustion.

"But at least for tonight we can head home a little early. It'll be nice to get our fill of sleep for once...Zero?"

Vampire hunters' senses are much sharper than those of a human being, and Zero had caught a glint of something moving fast out of the corner of his eye. A bare second later, Kaito noticed it as well.

"It's pretty close to us. Where is it, Zero? Can you tell?"

Zero's eyes were even sharper. The two scanned the area with heightened senses, sifting signs of their target from other sensory detail.

Zero said at last, "It's to the west. It's watching us from the shadow of that building."

"Damn. And here we'd just completed our orders for tonight!"

Their eyes meeting, the two hunters nodded silently to each other, and then without warning they simultaneously leapt to the attack. Realizing he'd been spotted, the vampire turned and fled.

"It's too late to run now!" Kaito called after the fleeing vampire as he gave chase. But the vampire was fast on his feet as well. Hoping to shake Kaito from his trail, he ran for a street corner that would take him briefly out of the hunters' line of sight. Wheeling sharply around the corner, he ducked into an alleyway, planning to slip away under the cover of darkness.

As the dark of the alley enveloped him, the vampire gave a sigh of relief. But he was immediately greeted by the unsettling sound of a gun being cocked. He looked up to see Zero—his grim face hard and determined—pointing a gun that had *Bloody Rose* inscribed on the barrel.

"Damn you!" The vampire scrambled backward, only to discover Kaito blocking his path.

"You saw us earlier, didn't you? Once we have our prey in our sights, it never gets away. Nothing gets past our stellar tag-team approach!" Kaito declared. "You shouldn't have underestimated us."

"Ah..."

With the vampire now trapped like a rat, Zero aimed *Bloody Rose* at his heart and advanced.

"What were you planning? Answer me."

"I-I was ordered to watch the two of you."

"Watch us? Why?"

"I-I don't know..."

Zero said nothing, but his finger moved subtly over the trigger. Catching the movement, the vampire's face paled.

"Wait, please! I honestly don't know anything!" He raised both his hands imploringly, trying to convey that he was no enemy. On the back of his hand was a tattoo of rose petals arranged in a crest. Behind him, Kaito frowned, his eyes puzzled as they fell on the tattoo.

"Red rose petals...You're a practitioner of some kind?"

"No, this is our leader's crest."

"Your leader's? Zero, do you know who he's talking about?"

His expression rigid, Zero nodded slightly.

"He means a certain red-and-purple-eyed woman with extremely bad taste."

The crowded streets were full of flirtatious voices, and the air stank of cigarettes and alcohol. It was a city where a constant hum of chaotic energy filled the air, and the nightlife never ended. Here people slept through the day. At night lamplight illuminated the town as if it were daylight. It was the kind of city that brought out one's worst vices. Here and there along the alleyways stood women posing outrageously in dresses that bared more skin than they covered, beckoning to customers in front of waiting brothels.

In the midst of such a city, Zero and Kaito made an eye-catching pair. The women in the alleyways called out to them, invitation plain in their eyes, but Zero strode on without sparing them a glance.

"H-hey, where are we going?" Kaito asked, walking quickly to keep up.

Zero said nothing. He then came to a stop in front of a certain bar in a back alley, opening the door without a moment's hesitation. In the bar's dim interior, unsavory-looking men sat about enjoying a round of drinks served by women in heavy makeup. The men took in the unfamiliar newcomers and demanded, "Who're you?" but Zero strode past them to the bar, paying them no heed.

"What'll you have?" asked the bartender.

"The Queen of the Abyss."

The bartender's eyes flickered toward his face for the barest of seconds before he lowered them and politely murmured, "One moment, please." He set about preparing the cocktail.

Seating himself on the stool beside Zero, Kaito looked at his partner in surprise. "Hey, aren't you underage?" he asked.

"Don't worry. It's not what you think."

Two cocktails in tall narrow glasses were soon placed before them. The drink's colorful contents went in a gradient from red to purple—red like the color of blood and a purple like the midnight sky.

Zero shifted his glass to the side to reveal the coaster beneath it. It was marked with the same rose crest they had seen on the vampire earlier. He wrote something on the coaster, flipped it over, and slid it back toward the bartender.

The bartender glanced at the writing on the coaster and said, "If you would please proceed..." indicating the back of the bar with his eyes. Leaving the cocktails untouched, Zero slid off his stool and headed where the bartender had indicated.

What the heck is this? Kaito wondered, following him. At the back of the shop, they were greeted by a man in a suit standing beside a closed door. The man opened it for them, and the pair made their way through to what should have been a VIP room. Instead a single candle illuminated a staircase that descended into darkness.

"So I'm guessing that at the bottom of these stairs, we'll find a woman with extremely bad taste?"

"Yeah."

"What is this, a secret hideout?" Kaito grumbled. "Does she think she's a supervillain or something?"

After descending the stairs, the pair found themselves in a room fragrant with the scent of roses. It was surprisingly spacious and airy for a room so deep underground. A great many roses in vases were placed decoratively about the room.

In the very center of the room, surrounded by a sea of roses, was a red velvet sofa. A woman sat upon it with her legs crossed. She indeed had mismatched eyes—one red, one purple—and she shifted in a way that showed the voluptuous breasts peeking out of her low neckline to fine advantage as she rose to stroll sultrily toward Zero.

"It's been a while, Zero."

With a face that said she already knew what he had come to ask, she placed a long, white finger under his chin and lifted it. Tilting her head so that her lips were so close to his ear that they might have brushed it, she whispered, "Have you fallen for my scent yet?"

"Of course not, Shien," he replied.

"Dear me. How could you say that now after pursuing me so intensely in the past?"

With a throaty laugh, Shien reached out a finger tipped

with a blood-red nail and pressed it softly to Zero's lips. Every inch of her body seemed to exude a poisonous sensuality. There was not a trace of innocence about her. She embodied womanly passion, and the burden of fleshly desires seemed to coil about her.

"My, aren't you a cold one?" She slid her finger from Zero's lips and pressed it back against her own mouth. Looking faintly irritated at the action, Zero continued staring her down.

Standing behind him to cover their retreat, a half-dazed Kaito mumbled, "Hey, Zero...you haven't lost interest in women, have you?"

Zero sighed in mild exasperation. "Don't get the wrong idea, Kaito."

Zero recalled his first meeting half a year ago with Shien, the woman with the red and purple eyes. It was back before he had learned to control the mad urges inside him. He had spent his days almost frantically hunting vampires, trying to lose himself in the work. During that period he had simply tried to run away from everything in order to survive.

Back then Shien had been living far removed from people in a safe house hidden deep in a forest. Standing before the ivy-covered mansion in the depths of the forest, Zero withdrew the photo of the target from his breast pocket and confirmed her particulars.

"Level C Vampire."

The beauty in the photo he'd received from the Hunter Society was named Shien—spelled with the Chinese characters for "purple" and "flame"—perhaps because of her strikingly colored eyes. Whether it was her real name or not was anyone's guess. On the back of the photo was all the information the society had on her. Shien apparently had been a pureblood's lover once. The wealth she had accumulated during that time now allowed her to live as she pleased.

"Hey! Who are you?!" A guard patrolling the safe house's perimeter had just spotted Zero. Not bothering to unholster *Bloody Rose*, Zero easily dispatched the man with a sharp kick.

One more swift blow to the head had him out cold.

Zero seized the unconscious man by the back of the neck and dragged him to the entrance of the house, throwing the doors open with his free hand.

Inside he found the first floor deserted. Before him a spiral staircase draped with a crimson-colored runner extended down into a basement. Deep red roses were placed decoratively about the room in various nooks and crannies, even twined around the gold-plated bannister and doorknobs.

The entire mansion was filled with the sweet scent of roses. But there was another smell even stronger than the roses that hung thickly in the air.

The basement, huh?

Zero tightened his grip on the guard's throat enough to ensure he was unconscious, then turned to brace his hands on the railing to leap nimbly over it in one swift movement. He landed lightly at the bottom of the stairs and found himself facing a door. Opening it, he was immediately assailed by an overpowering stench. Raising his sleeve to his nose, he scrunched up his face in disgust. This was no longer the fragrant scent of red roses in full bloom. It was the smell of something much redder and lusher with life.

What in the world is this?

Despite all he'd seen and experienced as a vampire hunter, even Zero was momentarily dumbfounded by the strangeness of the scene before him. There upon the floor of the wide room lay at least a dozen—no, perhaps several dozens of—youths and young men. And from every wrist oozed pools of blood.

At the very center of the landscape of living corpses, a gossamer curtain sectioned off a small area. Zero could sense the presence of a vampire within it. Stepping carefully around the bodies, Zero approached the gauzy curtain—translucent like a dragonfly wing—and tore it open.

"Dear me..."

In a tub filled with red water, Shien looked up from the feast she had been in the midst of consuming. Whether she had been aware of the intruder or not, she showed not the slightest sign of perturbance at his sudden appearance.

That isn't bathwater, Zero realized. *It's blood.*

It was a frightful sight. The woman had drained the blood of all these men to bathe in. Shien was like a rose that had bloomed from drinking human blood.

In a surprisingly sweet voice she said, "What an adorable boy we have here. Did you come here to offer your blood to me too?"

Her eyes never leaving Zero's, Shien reached for the young man kneeling beside her and lowered her lips to his throat, baring her fangs. Apparently dazed by her beauty, the man heedlessly offered himself to her.

"..."

Zero leveled his gun at her.

Shien gave him an empty smile from her glistening crimson lips. "A real vampire hunter came all this way just to kill me? I must be getting pretty famous."

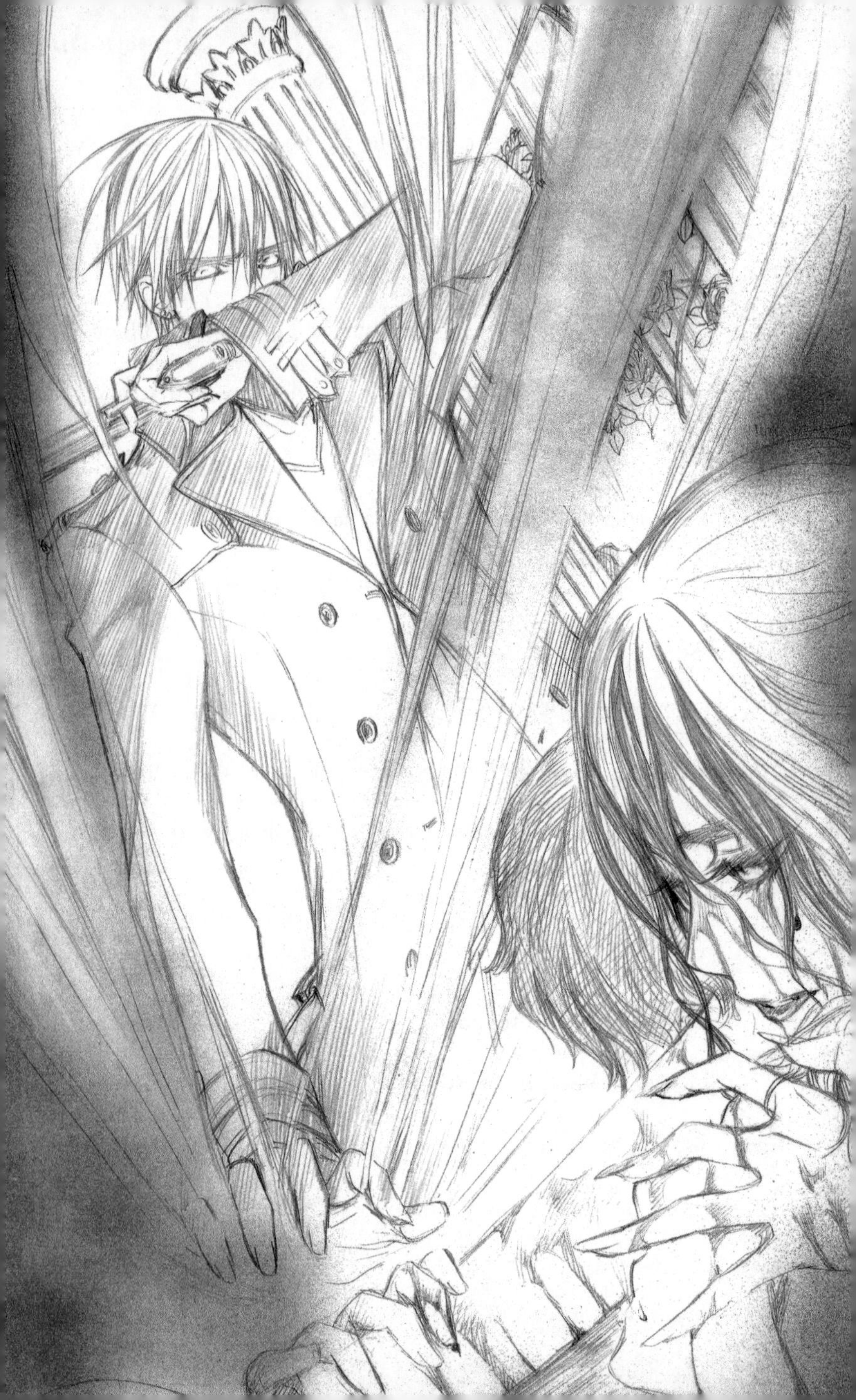

"Release that man right now."

The latest victim wrapped in Shien's arms had lost vast quantities of blood like the others scattered about the room. Zero could detect the faint breath of life still in him. He needed medical help immediately.

"How unfortunate," said Shien. "I can't say I enjoy being ordered around."

"Release him," Zero repeated. When he moved to tighten his finger around the trigger, Shien relented with a huff and a slight shrug of her shoulders.

"And here I was enjoying a special feast tonight...Oh well. Off you go."

"But Shien-sama..." the man protested weakly. Despite what she had just been doing to him, he continued to gaze at her with adoration as he obeyed.

"Now, little vampire hunter, why don't you turn around and give me a moment?"

"Why should I?" Fearing that she would attempt to flee,

Zero remained facing her.

"Well, if you want to see my naked body so much, I suppose I don't mind," Shien said, lifting herself gracefully from the bathtub. Her snowy white body dripping with blood stood completely bare and exposed before him.

Though Zero kept the arm pointing his gun steady and perfectly aligned with its mark, he averted his eyes slightly.

"You're more of a gentleman than I expected. What an adorable boy you are..." Laughing huskily, Shien rinsed herself clean with cold water.

"You can look now, my innocent little dear," she said.

Zero raised his eyes back to her and found her clad in a bathrobe. She let down her long hair. When she moved to push back a few stray locks from around her shoulders, the top of her robe shifted to show him a flash of ample breasts.

"Invading my lovely bath time...You certainly are an impatient boy."

"Enough with the innuendo," Zero snapped.

Shien sighed. "Fine. What now? What crimes are you charging me with?"

Zero pulled a small bottle from his pocket that was sealed with a crest of stylized rose petals. Inside the bottle was a dark red liquid that could have been taken for wine.

"Look familiar? It's produced by your organization."

"I know it is. So what?"

Even faced with proof of her crimes, Shien continued smiling languidly.

She's got guts, Zero thought. Or perhaps what lay at the depths of her was not so much guts as a bottomless abyss. *She's dangerous*, he thought.

Shien was still eyeing the bottle in his hand. "It can't quite compare to the Water of Life that's so popular among the aristocrats," she said, "but I'm told it's quite tasty in its own right."

"You acknowledge you are the head of this organization, correct?"

"Let me tell you this—I did not take any of these men's

blood by force. They offered it to me of their own free will. I took it as I might take money offered to me," Shien continued with perfect composure. "These are all perfectly legal activities. We've done nothing that merits my destruction at the hands of the Hunter Society."

"Do you really think excuses like that make any difference in the face of all this?" Zero gestured around him at the room littered with men nearing death.

"I already explained it to you, didn't I? These boys came to me. They wanted to be bitten by me. They said they would do absolutely anything to feel my bite. How could I ignore their poor little pleas? If you desire my bite too—"

"Don't be ridiculous!"

Reaching the end of his patience, Zero leveled *Bloody Rose* at her again. Though she must have known that a vampire hunter's weapon could kill her, Shien's composure remained unshaken.

"I can tell you're dying of thirst, dear boy. With all this

blood in the air, I wonder how long you'll be able to endure it. I don't know what circumstances led to your becoming one of our kind, but I do empathize with what you're going through."

"Meaning what?"

"We vampires can sate our eternal thirst only by drinking the blood of the one we love," she said. "It was the same for me as well. Since he fell into eternal slumber, neither my heart nor body has ever felt fully sated."

For a brief moment, Shien's eyes reflected real loneliness. Zero wondered if *that man* was the pureblood lover she once had.

Pureblood.

The moment he registered the word, the image of a certain girl's face flashed through his mind. She'd been beside him for so long. But there had been no choice but for him to leave her behind. Just thinking of Yuki made the conflicted emotions he had smothered away in his heart threaten to explode.

"I've had enough of your rubbish," Zero said, his voice low.

As he moved to pull the trigger, the thick scent of blood in the air finally overwhelmed him. His brain went numb for a split second, causing him to lose his footing.

Shien didn't waste her chance. Fast as lightning, her foot connected with the hand holding *Bloody Rose*.

"...!"

Caught off-guard by the sudden attack, Zero lost his grip on his gun. *Bloody Rose* crashed to the floor with a loud clang.

Zero realized he had lost his weapon when the thirst for blood overcame him. Shien, who had taken perfect advantage of his moment of weakness, now stood with one of her sharp, blood-red nails poised just above his jugular.

"I may not be armed, but I can still match you in a fight, boy. Don't underestimate me just because I'm a Level C vampire."

Shien pressed her nail lightly into Zero's throat, breaking the skin. Zero could feel blood begin to seep from the wound.

"Hm, what an interesting fragrance. It seems your blood is far from pure." Breathing in the scent of his blood deeply, Shien gave him a faint smirk.

"Shut up," Zero growled.

"Hee...Perhaps I'll make it so I'll never have to listen to your insolence ever again. Starting now." Shien dug her nail into his skin and brought her lips toward his throat. Refusing to retreat, Zero glared fiercely at her. Shien paused a bare breath away from him and peered into his eyes.

"Those eyes of yours, colored with such despair...they're lovely. Just looking at them sends shivers down my spine."

"..."

"What do you say? Want to join me?"

"What are you talking about?" Zero asked after a pause. Shien grinned, amused by his wariness.

"I mean," she explained, "even though sales of my blood are expanding and spreading throughout the underworld, in the end a vampire is a vampire. There are some who'll never be fully comfortable doing business with me."

"So what?"

"I want a contact in the Hunter Society."

"You mean me?"

"Yes. I'd be able to spare your life. And it would make me happy to count you as an ally."

"..."

Zero paused to consider the idea. His old self would have probably turned the offer down point-blank. There was no way he would have agreed to partner up with a vampire he had just met. However...

She's apparently got a sizable information network, plus personal connections throughout the vampire realm. She's far more embedded than any non-vampire could ever hope to be. Maybe I can make use of her, he thought.

As a pureblood's lover for many years, Shien's information network would be vast indeed, and her web of informants everywhere.

"It's not a terrible proposition," Zero said at length. At his assent, Shien withdrew her hand and licked the smeared blood off her extended fingertips. She wore a satisfied smile on her lips.

"Ah...Just as I thought, you have quite an interesting flavor. Now shall we begin the ritual to seal our oath?"

"Ritual?"

Zero shrank back slightly, making the sort of face a little boy might at having to dress up for a formal event of some kind. Shien huffed softly and smiled at him as if he were a sulking younger brother.

"Don't tell me you expect me to trust your word alone, dear boy? It does no good to either party if these sorts of things aren't formalized properly."

"So what do you want? My signature on a contract? Because that's not happening."

"Ha ha ha! Oh, I wouldn't do something so ludicrous as leave an inconvenient paper trail," she said. Her mirthful expression changed to one of invitation, and she wrapped her arms around Zero's neck. "You're thirsty, aren't you?" she murmured.

Her beauty was suddenly overwhelming. An overpowering scent of roses filled the air around them, making Zero's head reel. It was nearly nauseating. With her arms still wrapped around him, Shien raised one hand and began running it softly through his hair.

"Drink my blood, dear boy..."

Entranced, Zero was on the verge of doing just that when he managed to pull himself back. His voice dropped as he muttered sullenly, "Don't call me 'boy.'"

As soon as he had finished speaking, Shien grasped his hair and pulled his head down to her neck. From that time on, Zero and Shien were linked.

"Well, well! So you've actually laid hands on another woman, huh?"

Having heard the full story, Kaito gave his friend an impressed whistle to tease him. Now Kaito, Zero, and Shien sat across from one another at a table in a guest parlor where the smell of blood was less pungent. Shien shifted, crossing her shapely legs again. It was a habit designed to draw attention to them.

"Oh? So Zero has a special someone, does he?"

"Yeah. She's a flat-chested slip of a girl." Kaito grinned.

Shien chuckled. "In that case, I'm jealous. Well then, Zero, what is this mission of yours that was so important you had to bring your handsome senior hunter along with you? It's nothing good, I imagine?"

Kaito smirked and shrugged lightly at Zero's side. "Seems like you already know all about me, so I guess there's no point introducing myself."

Zero focused his attention on Shien and asked bluntly, "Shien, what are you sticking your nose into?"

"Impatient as always, I see." Shien sighed. "Things need to unravel at their own pace, you hear? It won't do for you to rush headlong through everything in life."

"There's no point in trying to avoid the issue," Zero said. "Tell me what you want so badly that you went out of your way to annoy me by sending lackeys to keep tabs on me."

"I just wanted to ask you about something. It actually involves your senior hunter here too."

Having occupied the role of the outsider until now, Kaito looked at Shien in surprise. Shien smiled and went on to explain. "Both of you were present on that occasion, I believe? That rather infamous soirée where all manner of disturbances occurred?"

There was only one soirée she could have meant—the one Kaname Kuran had recently hosted. Many things had happened that night. It had been the society debut for Kuran's younger sister, Yuki. Somehow Yuki's friend—a human girl—had wound up there in the midst of a room full of vampires, igniting their lust for blood.

But the disturbances hadn't ended there. During the party the remains of the pureblood Ouri had been discovered in an empty room. How could something so sinister have happened at the event under everyone's noses?

The mystery surrounding Ouri's death only grew after it was officially declared to be a suicide. It was said the pureblood had taken one of the vampire hunters hired to guard the event and made her into his servant. He then commanded her to kill him with her anti-vampire weapon.

There were only a few purebloods present at the soirée: Kaname and Yuki Kuran as the hosts, and Sara Shirabuki, Ouri's fiancée. Though they were all under suspicion at the time, in the end no one could determine a motive that any of them would have for murdering Ouri.

But there were many who still believed it had not been a suicide. Zero and Kaito were counted among them. And though they had not spoken directly about it, Zero knew that Yuki did not believe it either.

Yuki...

Zero's mind immediately summoned up the memory of

Yuki from that night—her face soft and somber. Just as soon as the image surfaced, Zero buried the emotions associated with it deep in his chest.

Turning his focus back on Shien, he asked, "Are you saying your information network turned up some new information about the case?"

Shien smiled again. "Let's agree to some terms of exchange before we continue, shall we? If you're willing to accept my little request, I will tell you all that I've learned about the incident."

Her smile widening, Shien raised a red-tipped finger to her mouth and pressed it coyly against her plush lips.

The heady scent of wine and women pervaded the city. Drunk on it, men stumbled through the night, indulging their desires and seeking new vices, knowing all the while that the passions they sought could lead to their demise like moths that drew too close to the lights illuminating the dark.

Tonight Shien was entertaining the chief executive of a new startup company that had shot to fame overnight by developing a synthetic designer fabric that had become all the rage in the apparel industry. Still in his twenties, the man cut a fine figure in his designer suit as he raised Shien's hand to his lips and kissed it with perfect poise.

"You look even more radiant than usual tonight," he said. "Every jewel in this world would pale beside the brilliance of your eyes."

"Oh, you flatterer!" Shien accepted his impassioned greeting deftly, shrugging delicately out of her *haori*. The man stepped forward to take it from her smoothly. In doing so he noticed Zero and Kaito standing on either side of the door.

"And who are they?" he asked Shien.

"Just some new toys of mine," she said lightly. "Pay them no mind."

The venue chosen to conduct tonight's business was a private room in a casino reserved for VIPs only. The dress code

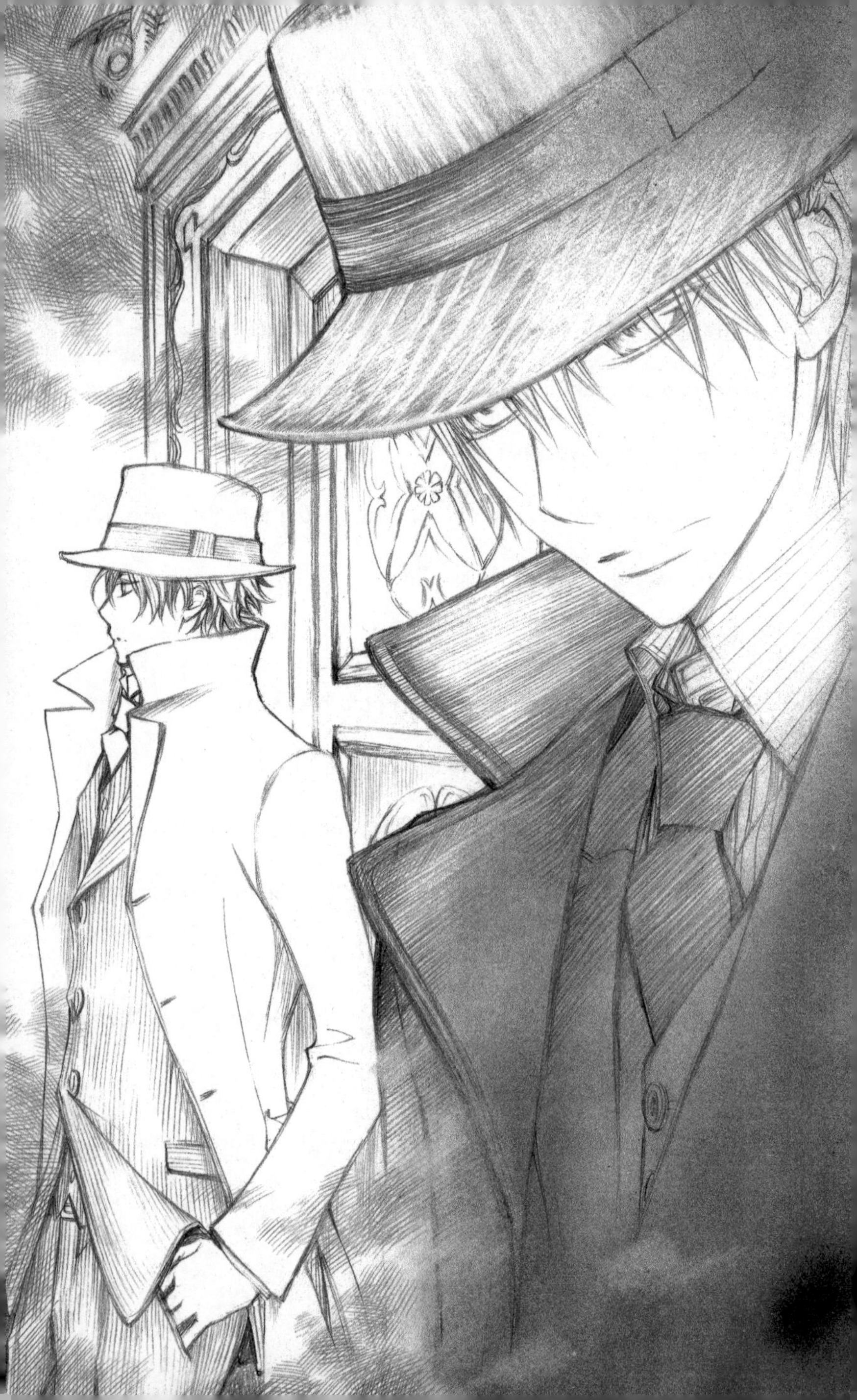

was black tie for those who had been invited in. The staff was dressed sharply in black as well.

One such staff member entered bearing a top-grade bottle of wine, which was quickly opened for a toast by Shien and her guest. After drinks and light flirtation, the man's arm found its way around Shien's waist. With a bewitching smile on her lips, Shien allowed the arm to stay where it was.

Though she made a great show of caressing and flirting with the man, Zero and Kaito noticed that her eyes—which remained quite cool and collected—were carefully scanning and cataloging the man from head to toe. When she playfully undid his tie, they could see she also was checking for concealed weapons.

With his shirt collar wide open now, Shien lowered her lips to the exposed skin of his chest. He, in turn, slid a hand into her cleavage. Shien gave an alluring sigh in response and signaled subtly to her two guards to exit the room.

As soon as they'd made their silent retreat into the hallway,

Kaito grumbled, "That woman doesn't need guards to protect her as far as I can tell." He went on complaining in a similar vein under his breath, but Zero could see Kaito was continually scanning the hallway and the exits nonetheless. There were still external threats to watch for. Zero kept an alert eye to their surroundings despite leaning in a casual pose against the wall.

This had been Shien's request in exchange for her information: she'd wanted them to guard her.

"The truth is, someone appears to be targeting my life..."

Poison had been found in her food, and there had been a small house fire along with various traffic accidents caused by mysterious malfunctions in the cars she was riding in. The attempts on Shien's life had continued until a few of the "dear boys" serving as her guards had wound up injured—and one dead. This had spurred Shien into action to eliminate her unknown enemy.

The incident had occurred on a night when Shien's business negotiations with a lover had wound up running so long that she decided to stay the night with him. Her current favorite "dear boy" had been serving as her escort that night, so she had sent him back to the safehouse ahead of her. But the car's steering suddenly locked up on his drive home, causing the car to go straight off a cliff. Had Shien gone home that night as planned, she would have been in that car too...

"I suppose I'm not horribly surprised someone might bear enough of a grudge against me to want me dead. But unfortunately for them, I have no intention of letting myself be bumped off. And I would hate for more of my boys to get caught in the crossfire."

"That's why you want us to guard you?"

"Two dangerous vampire hunters serving as my personal bodyguards? I couldn't ask for better protectors, could I?"

Their main job would be to keep Shien safe from more attempts on her life. If the culprit wound up being a vampire, they would hunt him as was their job. If he was human, he would not be killed. Zero had been careful to include this provision when he'd accepted Shien's deal.

This was how Zero and Kaito found themselves in their present situation.

"Seriously, how many lovers does that woman have anyway?" Kaito complained. If his expression was a bit weary, Zero couldn't blame him. Just who could be targeting Shien? Without a single clue to go on, Shien had insisted their best course of action was to simply accompany her wherever she went. For the past several days Zero and Kaito had followed her all over town as she went about her business. But so far nothing had happened, and the fatigue was starting to show on the faces of the two hunters as they trailed Shien on her endless nighttime romps about the city.

"Well, I'm guessing the guy we want isn't Mr. CEO in there," Kaito said. "He doesn't look like he'd have the guts to kill anyone. I bet he just wants to make use of that woman's information network."

Kaito carried on making snide remarks while remaining

alert. It didn't surprise Zero that Kaito's personality didn't take well to Shien's. Kaito had always been a straightforward guy, blunt and uncomplicated in determining right from wrong in the world.

He really hasn't changed at all since I first met him, Zero thought.

Shien must have sensed it as well. She hadn't attempted to lay a finger on Kaito since they'd met. Or perhaps she understood that Zero would kill her on the spot if she ever tried.

A soft voice spoke.

"Excuse me?"

A young man had appeared before the pair. He was Kaede, one of Shien's "dear boys." He had become a special favorite of hers recently and was currently serving as her chauffeur.

Kaede had a willowy build. It made him look fairly harmless, but beneath his well-cut suit, his toned body housed a fair amount of muscle. Zero suspected that he served Shien not just as a driver but also as her bodyguard when she was on the road.

"What is it?"

"I just wondered if Mistress Shien was—"

"She's still inside," Kaito said, jerking his thumb over his shoulder at the closed door.

It was little wonder that Kaede should feel anxious for Shien with the trail of unfortunate incidents plaguing her lately. He glanced at the door, an uneasy look on his face.

"Ooh..."

Shien's husky moan was audible through the door. Kaito scowled.

"Just how long are they going to do it?" he muttered.

"Kaito," Zero cautioned, "if you're going to complain about everything, you'll start annoying me too."

"Right, sorry. But don't act like you're the adult here!" Kaito clucked his tongue disapprovingly. Kaede's shoulders stiffened.

"You both misunderstand Mistress Shien," he spoke up suddenly. "This is all strictly for business. She had no other purpose for..."

Catching himself, Kaede paused and said more composedly, "I beg your pardon. I've overstepped myself." His face smoothed back into its habitual calm. "It seems tonight's business hasn't quite ended yet. When Mistress Shien emerges, will you please tell her I switched cars to be safe?"

"And you've checked the new car?"

"Of course. I scanned it for wiretaps, bombs, and any other suspicious materials. It's clean."

"Okay then. Thanks."

Kaede nodded. "I'll be waiting with the car."

But even after he had gone, it was a long while before Shien finally emerged from the room. Apparently tonight's negotiations had gone exceptionally well.

A rumor began to spread throughout the city.

"Shien has hired two new bodyguards."

The news was so widespread that even Shien's hidden

nemesis seemed to be proceeding with caution; he made no further attempts on her. But as the days passed and nothing continued to happen, Kaito became more irritable and looked increasingly fed up as Shien continued to drag them to her liaisons each night.

"You don't think that woman's just trying to drag us little by little into becoming her permanent bodyguards, do you?" he said one night. "Because if that's the case, I would've been better off staying a teacher."

"You enjoyed teaching?" Zero asked in surprise. "That's unexpected."

"Is it?" Kaito shrugged. "You know, there were students who said to me, 'Your lectures are really easy to understand, Mr. Takamiya!' Stuff like that. Well, not that you would know. You were always asleep in class."

The two went on exchanging jovial insults until Shien arrived for their nightly business. Her face was unusually grim as she got in the car.

"I'm meeting a somewhat troublesome customer tonight," she explained.

"Lady, you don't meet anyone but troublesome customers," Kaito quipped from the passenger's seat.

"You certainly have a smart mouth on you, young man," Shien said with a small smirk. "Though I do love men with ash-brown hair like yours. Can't you be well-mannered like Zero?" Shien scooted closer to Zero, who was seated beside her in the backseat. She snuggled against his arm flirtatiously. Though Zero refrained from pushing her away, his shoulders stiffened noticeably and his expression showed his irritation.

"So what are you dealing today? Drugs? Weapons?" Zero asked.

"I'll tell you in detail if you really want to know. But are you sure you won't get angry?"

"In that case I'll pass."

Kaede, who was serving again as driver tonight, spoke up. "Mistress Shien, we've reached our destination."

He stopped the car at the entrance to an abandoned warehouse. When Kaito got out and opened the rear door for Shien, Kaede had already hurried around the other side of the car in time to offer his hand to her in assistance. It seemed he was determined not to lose his role as Shien's escort to anyone else just yet. Shien gave a husky chuckle in recognition of it as she placed her hand in Kaede's.

I guess he's deep under this woman's spell just like all the rest of them, Kaito thought. Kaito and Zero considered Kaede to be calmer and more reasonable than the rest of his "dear boy" brethren. But apparently that was not the case.

"Looks like the other party isn't here yet," Zero commented as he alighted from the car's other side and looked around the entrance to the warehouse. The team of underlings who had been sent on ahead to ensure the building was secure emerged from the front doors, giving them the thumbs-up sign. The signal meant the building was all clear—no bombs had been found.

"Hmph. Guess nothing's gonna happen tonight either," Kaito said with a small cluck of his tongue. He snapped the car door shut.

Not long after entering the warehouse, they heard Shien's buyer pulling up outside. He was an infamous syndicate leader in the criminal underworld, and Zero and Kaito—not wanting to be seen associating with him—pulled the brims of their hats down lower to hide their faces.

The man strode into the warehouse at the head of his cluster of bodyguards. His body was stocky and muscular—the exact opposite of the "dear boys" Shien favored. It seemed this particular transaction would not develop into anything more than business.

"How rude of me to make a lady wait," he said, flashing Shien a white smile. "My deepest apologies. I got so excited knowing I was going to see you that I wound up taking more time getting dressed up for you. Let me make my apologies properly."

He reverently took Shien's hand and pressed it gently to his lips. While his head was bowed, Shien took the opportunity to let a small crease of distaste furrow her brow just lightly enough so that the man's underlings wouldn't notice.

"So *that's* what she meant by a troublesome customer, huh?" Kaito whispered.

"At least this means we'll probably get to go home early tonight," Zero replied.

Under the watchful eyes of the vampire hunters, the deal proceeded smoothly to completion.

"That should do it," Shien said in conclusion.

"Yes," the man said, "but there's no need for us to linger in such a gloomy place. I'd be honored if you would join me for dinner at my estate—"

"I'm so sorry," Shien crooned, cutting smoothly into the invitation, "but I already have another engagement scheduled tonight." With that she turned swiftly on her heel and strode toward the exit.

Then it happened.

CLANG!

Something metallic rolled across the floor.

For a moment, every occupant of the room could only stare at it in surprise. Then, with a roar like crashing thunder, a blinding light filled the room.

A bomb?!

After the dust settled, Kaito slowly raised his head. He had Shien wrapped securely in his arms as she coughed to clear her lungs of dust. She seemed unhurt overall. Being the one standing closest to her when the bomb went off, Kaito had instinctively grabbed her and leapt behind the nearest bit of cover he could find. His instincts had saved their lives.

"What is the meaning of this?!" Across the room, Shien's buyer and his retainers were in a rage. Kaito ignored them and picked himself up off of Shien, glancing around to assess the situation. The dust and debris in the air were starting to clear, and thanks to some faint illumination from outside he could make out most of the scene within the warehouse. The bomb had thankfully been a small one, and its blast power had been fairly limited.

"Looks like their big boss over there is all right," he said to Shien. "I take it they're probably not strangers to stuff like this either."

Any black-market deal was rife with danger. Kaito knew that anyone who survived long in the criminal underworld was used to facing the threat of violence and probably much worse. Judging by how well his bodyguards had reacted to protect him, they were seasoned pros when it came to this sort of thing.

I guess humans in this business have no choice but to pay good money for bodyguards, he thought. Kaito glanced back over to see how Shien's underlings had fared. Those who had been standing nearest the door were gone, presumably giving chase to whomever had thrown the bomb into the warehouse.

Wait... Where's Zero?

Kaito glanced quickly around him, but Zero was nowhere

to be found. As he was wondering where his partner could have gone, Shien's buyer stormed up to him.

"Hey! I don't know what you people think you're playing at—"

"Aren't you the one who's playing?" Shien's calm voice interjected smoothly. She emerged from the cover that Kaito had provided, still smiling with perfect composure. It wasn't an unnatural attitude to have for one who had had nothing to do with the explosion. But it rubbed her business companion the wrong way.

"Don't think you can play coy with me just because you've got a pretty face! What was that supposed to be? An attempt to take over my new smuggling route for weapons?"

"Oh, is that what you think this was?" Shien shrugged languidly. "I couldn't care less about your smuggling route."

"Don't you lie to me!"

"I'm not lying. I detest seeing blood spilled in any ugly manner. Do you imagine I'd have the slightest wish to involve myself with matters such as these?"

"You think you can play your little games with me?!" The man pulled a gun from his breast pocket and pointed it at Shien. Kaito instantly appeared between them, giving the enraged mob boss an unimpressed look.

"My, my," Shien said, giving her vampire hunter bodyguard an appreciative glance.

"I know that gun isn't going to kill a woman like you, but as your bodyguard this isn't the sort of thing I can allow," Kaito said over his shoulder to Shien, his eyes never leaving the gun.

Shien fixed her aggressor with a stony look. "You were behind the attempts on my life all along, correct?"

"Lady, I don't know what you're talking about. We're partners in business transactions, so why would I—"

"Business transactions? Is that what you call your little invitations for backroom negotiations with me?'"

"W-what?!" In a mortified rage, the man made to pull the trigger. A voice cut through the air.

"Hold it."

Zero stood in the entrance of the warehouse with a hand clamped firmly on the arm of a young man he had pulled inside.

"The one who threw the bomb just now—and the one responsible for your malfunctioning cars and poisoned food— is this guy."

The group strained to make out the man's face in the faint light.

"Kaede?!" Shien gasped. "How could you think one of my boys is responsible for this?"

"Mistress Shien!" Kaede cried, his face wretched. "It's because you kept favoring other men over me! I've given you everything—my body, my heart, my very soul! And yet you...you wouldn't look only at me...That's why I..."

Kaede, despairing of ever obtaining Shien's affections exclusively, had begun a campaign to remove the other "dear boys" from Shien's life.

Meaning...

...the ones he was trying to target tonight were actually the two of us...

Zero and Kaito exchanged an exasperated look. But at least the culprit had been unmasked, and their guard duties were finally at an end.

The next day Zero found himself strolling through the little city at night. At a certain establishment in a certain back alley, he found Shien already seated and waiting for him at the bar.

"You actually went out of your way to come see me?" he asked.

"I did. I thought we could share a toast, dear boy." Shien smiled, and two cocktails instantly appeared before them. The drinks were two-toned, shifting in color halfway up the glass from red to purple. Shien reached out and raised her "Queen of the Abyss."

"And where is that darling senior hunter tonight?"

"If you mean Kaito, he's off on a different assignment."

"I see. That's a shame. I wanted to thank him for saving me yesterday," Shien said, sipping her cocktail. Feeling no inclination to do likewise, Zero subtly pushed his glass away from him.

"What did you do with Kaede?" he asked. Normally Zero would have taken him in and had the Hunter Society determine a proper punishment. But this time he felt that leaving him to Shien would serve just as well. The important thing was that he and Kaito had upheld their end of the bargain.

"Oh, I made sure he received a proper punishment," Shien said. "I didn't kill him, of course. But let's say he's had all the tough love he can handle for now. In a way I suppose he got what he really wanted in the end." She idly swilled the colorful contents of her glass around.

Not wanting to pry deeper into the details of Kaede's "loving" punishment, Zero cut straight to the punch.

"So as you requested, we caught the one responsible

for the incidents. Now it's time for you to uphold your end of the bargain."

Shien had promised him new information related to Ouri's case. That had been the only reason Zero and Kaito had agreed to help her.

Zero asked, "Did you have some kind of connection to the pureblood who died at the soirée?" That wouldn't surprise him. She had been a part of the purebloods' society once.

Shien grinned. "That would have been interesting, wouldn't it? But unfortunately no."

"Then how did you wind up learning this new information?"

"I looked into it," Shien replied. "In the world of business, you never know what events may or may not affect your dealings, so you keep informed."

"Meaning you like to keep your deck stacked with trump cards for later use?" Zero said flatly. *She really is a dangerous woman,* he thought.

"Very much so. For instance, the connection between you

and the Kuran princess..."

Zero glanced at her sharply, a glare of warning in his eyes. Shien smiled serenely back at him and shrugged.

"My, it seems she's even more important to you than I'd guessed. Though it really isn't much of a trump card. It's common knowledge that you and the Kuran princess were raised together by the head of the Hunter Society, after all."

"..."

Shien chuckled. "All right, I suppose I've teased you enough for now." She downed the rest of her cocktail, then flipped over the coaster it had been sitting on. A school's name and address appeared.

"Recently the mayor of the neighboring town hosted a party for his election committee. At the party he boasted that he had gained a connection with a pureblood vampire princess. He said he'd even gotten her admitted to Dahlia Girls Academy."

"A pureblood vampire princess...Sara Shirabuki, I'm guessing?" Zero said with a shrug. There had been only two pureblood princesses in attendance at the soirée—Yuki Cross and Sara Shirabuki. Zero was certain Yuki would never leave Kaname Kuran's side to go to some school that wasn't Cross Academy. By process of elimination, Shien could have meant only Sara Shirabuki. "Why would you bother researching her?"

"Because any information involving a pureblood is extremely useful. Everyone in the vampire realm knows that," said Shien. "Though if you're clumsy when trying to get close to them, you're in for a world of pain," she added.

That was why when the chance arose, Shien had made sure to get close to the purebloods. And as soon as that opportunity ended, she was quick to remove herself from their circle. This was the cynical rule by which this Level C vampire determined to get ahead had lived.

"It was really Sara Shirabuki who killed him, I believe?" she said at last.

"It seems extremely likely. But we have no proof."

Zero slipped the coaster with the address on it into his

breast pocket.

"Sara Shirabuki...Do you know what she means to do at Dahlia Academy?"

"That I don't know. I'm certain she's planning something," Shien murmured, as though talking to herself. "The victim was Sara Shirabuki's fiancé, wasn't he? Maybe she did it because she was in love with someone else."

"Huh?"

"Either that or perhaps he was getting in the way of some other plan of hers? Well, there are endless possible explanations." She gave Zero another light smile. "That's everything I can tell you about that. But if you get lonely, do come and see me again."

"As though I would come to this hellhole if I didn't have to."

"Cold as always, I see." Shien reached over and lightly poked Zero's cheek with the tip of her finger. She was truly a woman whose allure made men succumb. And just like poison, she couldn't help but ruin anyone she touched. Shien—a rare beauty whose charm was as fathomless as a bottomless abyss.

In a honeyed voice she said softly, "You really so interest me, you know. If you ever find yourself wanting me, I promise I'll be gentle with you, my adorable boy."

Dahlia Girls Academy lay in a quiet neighborhood at the top of a hill. A prestigious school with a storied past, its campus looked like a collection of noblemen's estates. It made the perfect backdrop for magazine photo shoots.

When Zero and Kaito arrived, they came across vampires familiar to them. Senri Shiki and Rima Toya were there working as models on a shoot for a fashion magazine. The pair of them were clad in school uniforms, wilting sleepily on a bench together. They were perhaps meant to portray a pair of students skipping class to doze in the sun.

Zero and Kaito had no interest in the photo shoot. They passed it by swiftly and headed for the school buildings. Zero could sense a certain aura within.

"There are vampires here," he muttered. "And I don't mean the modeling duo out there."

He could sense two of them within the school—most likely Takuma Ichijo and Sara Shirabuki.

"Looks like our intel was right on the money," Kaito muttered. Shien's information had been accurate. After confirming it, they had used the Hunter Society's resources to discover that Sara was posing as Ichijo's younger sister for some reason. They had come to gather intel.

Zero turned to his partner. "I'm going to go find out what she wants here."

Kaito nodded. "Yeah. Go for it."

They stood on a sky bridge that connected one school building to the next. Far below it ran a cobblestone path, winding out of sight. Zero leapt over the bridge's rail and landed lightly on the path below. Kaito gave a small sigh as he watched.

"Once he catches scent of prey, he's always full-speed ahead, isn't he? I don't know if he's just passionate about his work or if he's trying to make up for being a vampire..."

Zero himself was yet unable to explain his own reasoning for his current actions. A complex mess of emotions and blood-drenched memories still filled his mind. There was really only one thing he was certain of—his unwavering feelings for the girl who bore the name "tender princess."

A MAIDEN'S
MELANCHOLY

I was enjoying a marvelous breakfast one morning when...

"Why hello! Isn't this a fine morning?" came a voice. Head-master Cross had just entered my stall—that is, my lovely room—and was smiling broadly. He came over to me and said, "There's something I wish to speak with you about."

He was being unusually formal, so I paused from eating my breakfast and looked up at his face.

Oh my, what is it now? If you're going to tell me again to play nice and think I'll let the students ride me, you've got another thing coming! It's their fault for not being able to handle me the way Zero does.

Equestrian classes are very popular at Cross Academy. However, there is one thing about them all the students fear, and that is *me*, the maiden of the snowy hued blossoms. My name is White Lily! And it seems I've earned the unfortunate reputation of being a "wild horse." Honestly!

Well yes, I may have thrown a few students during class yesterday, but what of it? I thought to the headmaster. *They didn't show me proper respect as a lady, so of course I would have kicked them around a bit!*

When I turned my head huffily away from him, Headmaster Cross said placatingly, "There, there, now. Calm down," and then proceeded to tell me something utterly shocking.

"The truth is I've been up to some matchmaking," he said. "I've come to propose a match for you."

A match?!

As I stood there wide-eyed in shock, Headmaster Cross slipped nimbly into my line of sight and brandished a photo of my intended.

"This handsome gentleman is Black Sword! He's currently active on the racing circuit. He's quite famous for his speed among racehorses."

The horse in the photo had a strong, toned physique and a lustrous black coat. The photo must have been taken just after he had won a race, as he was bedecked with a flashy ornamental bridle. He stood posing proudly beside his jockey.

"His owner is eager to have him breed with a mare of such excellent pedigree as you, White Lily. Black Sword seemed quite interested as well when he was shown a photograph of you."

Oh really? I thought. *I am quite beautiful, of course. It's only natural that he would fall for me at first sight!*

"What do you think?" asked Headmaster Cross. "Would you like to meet him?"

Meet him?! Certainly not!

"*Neigh!*" I said and whirled sullenly away from him and kicked the photograph out of his hands with my back leg.

"Oh no! Not the precious matchmaking photograph!" he

wailed. As he turned to desperately grab at the airborne photograph, I gave his bum a little kick as well.

"Whoa!"

Oh please. That photo isn't precious. You should burn it or toss it in the trash! Never bring it into my presence again!

Allowing my aura of supreme irritation to blaze, I snorted loudly and pawed the ground with my front leg in defiance.

Headmaster Cross stood slowly, gingerly rubbing his rear and clutching the photograph to his chest.

"A-anyway," he said, "your matchmaking meeting with Black Sword is scheduled for one week from now!" And with that he all but fled from the stables.

Don't go around deciding my mates for me! I thought angrily after him. *I refuse to fall for any arranged match!*

I was in a foul mood for the rest of the day. Forcing me into a match without warning...Does he have no regard at all for my feelings?!

As I snorted in anger and stomped around in my room, a male student with an anxious expression on his face called out to me.

"E-excuse me, White Lily. Would you please allow me to ride you?"

This boy was trying to rope me into an equestrian class at a time like this?! I was enraged. Even when I wasn't heartily annoyed, I had never deigned to let anyone but Zero ride me!

Away with you, peasant! I'm in no mood for you! I shoved him aside with my nose and took off for the horse yard.

"W-wait, please!" he cried after me. "If I can't ride you, I'll be in trouble!"

If you want to ride me so badly, go become a real man like Zero!

And with that I made to return to my room when another male student stepped in my path.

"Today I am going to ride you for sure!" he declared. "Our grades depend on it! So please let us ride you!"

"Pretty please, White Lily!" cried the first boy, catching up with me from behind.

Honestly, chasing down a helpless maiden and trying to corner me? You scoundrels!

As the two of them hedged me in, I felt on the edge of panic.

No! I won't let you force yourselves on me, you beasts!

I whirled around and kicked out with my back legs.

Take this! Lily Kick!

My elegant attack knocked the pair of them away.

"Oof!"

"Gah!"

That's right! Don't you dare underestimate the great White Lily! I thought, tossing my mane.

There was a group of students watching us from a distance. I could hear one whispering, "Two more sacrificed." And another: "There goes that wild horse again!"

It hurt my feelings. How could they call me wild? I'm not

the one at fault here. The blame is with those students who are trying to bully me!

Everyone always misunderstands me! Poor me...I'm going to start crying...No one ever understands my pain! I heaved a deep sigh and then spotted—

Zero!

Zero was walking toward me, cutting a path straight through the throng of students.

Oh, Zero! I've missed you so much!

He rubbed my nose and gave me what I know to be a loving gaze.

"Are you at it again?" he asked.

Zero, listen to me! I thought at him. *Those students were bullying me! I was so scared, but I made myself be brave and I fought them off!*

"You never change, do you?"

That's right! It's been so dreadful to have to keep fighting off all these men who constantly come after me!

As Zero stroked my mane, he glanced over at the pair of boys who were picking themselves up off the ground and rubbing their sore behinds.

"Hard luck," he said to them.

Honestly, Zero, you're just too nice to them! I thought to him. *Don't feel sorry for them! They're the ones at fault here!*

As I snorted in annoyance, the boys stared at us.

"Hey, White Lily is nuzzling Kiryu!"

"You're amazing, Kiryu..."

I could hear them whisper. "He's the only one White Lily will acknowledge." "He really is the strongest guy at school."

I could hear them whispering on in that manner.

Of course he is! I thought. *I wouldn't let anyone I didn't acknowledge ride me. Zero's the only one here who's special!*

While keeping their distance, the boys watched Zero with respect. It made me feel so proud.

Zero's sleeping face is so sweet...

I stood beside Zero as he napped on a bale of hay, sneaking peeks at him as he slept. Such silky-soft hair...Those long, thick eyelashes...His long, slender fingers...Honestly, there was no part of him I didn't utterly adore.

He looks so comfortable right now...

Zero sometimes cut class and came to hang out with me like this.

I really am a naughty girl, aren't I? I thought. *Luring poor Zero out here with my irresistible beauty.*

I do want him to concentrate on his studies and do well, but when I think about how he takes the trouble to come out here and see me specially...Well, I just can't bring myself to turn him away. The time we spend together like this—just the two of us—is truly blissful.

Please let Zero always love me like this. Because I truly love him too! So even if I am doing wrong in keeping him here, I just can't make myself let go of these happy times...

"Neigh..."

In my sweet melancholy, I'd unconsciously whickered out loud. Zero stirred and cracked his eyes open a slit.

"Hm?"

Oh, I'm sorry, Zero! Did I wake you?

Zero glanced around him drowsily and then said to me, "The headmaster told me you were going to a matchmaking meeting tomorrow?"

W-well, I...

"He told me to scold you into behaving. Can you believe his nerve?"

Oh, Headmaster Cross! How could you order Zero to do such a thing? You're so mean! I'm so glad Zero agrees with me. We're definitely opposed to this match, aren't we, Zero? They'll have to wait a million years more before trying to tear us apart!

Zero and I met long ago, back when I was just a yearling. I had been brought to Cross Academy only recently, and he would often come to take care of me. He'd gallantly feed me milk or change my hay.

I wonder when it was that I began to yearn for him...

I suppose it was only natural that I eventually fell for his charms. I've always felt he was my destiny.

Zero was just a child back then, but now he's grown up to become a fine gentleman. And I too have become a lady...

It's true he's taciturn and a bit blunt at times, but I consider those things to be part of his charm. People who prattle on needlessly annoy me. I suppose it's true that a proper gentleman speaks his feelings only when absolutely necessary.

I wonder if he'll ever say he loves me...

Just the thought of it makes my heart pound.

Oh, no! No, I mustn't dream of a love confession so soon! He hasn't even told me he likes me yet!

"*Neigh, neigh!*"

"What are you getting so excited about all of a sudden? You're making it hard for me to sleep..."

O-oh, sorry! I just got so stirred up thinking about the two of

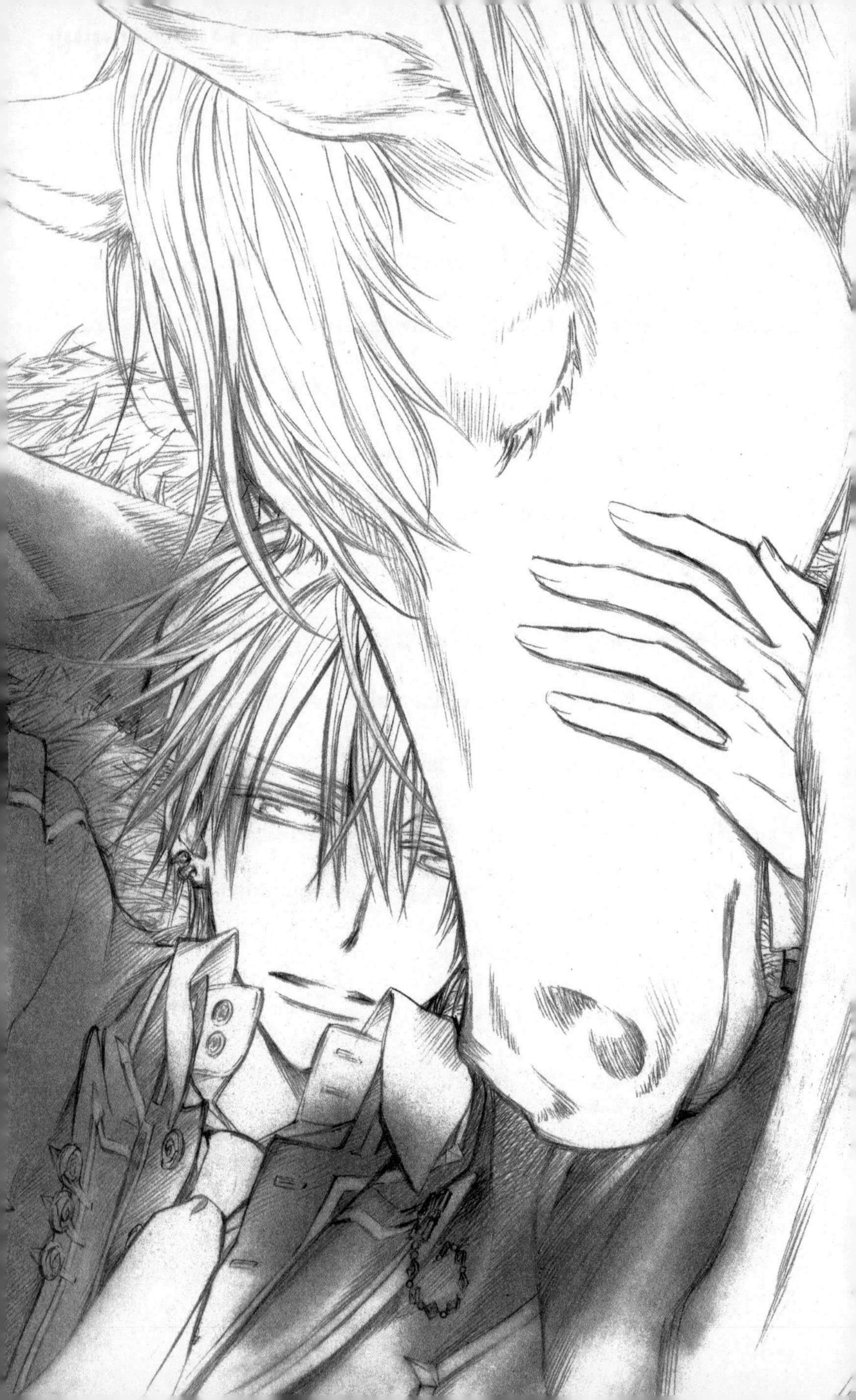

us...But never mind that! You can rest easy, Zero. I promise I won't go to any stupid matchmaking meeting!

But the moment I'd thought that to him, he said, "Well, you're the right age for a match. You should go for it..."

What?!

My ears must have deceived me.

Wait, what did you just say?

I nudged Zero's shoulder with my nose.

Zero, don't ignore me! Answer me!

"Stop it. I'm sleepy..." he murmured. He pushed my nose away and turned his back on me, his breathing growing long and deep.

What are you saying?! You're fine with me going off and marrying someone else?!

Zero's callous attitude made my heart clench painfully in my chest.

Zero, you dummy! Why are you being so cold to me all of a sudden?!

After all we'd been through, after how close we'd always been! I had sincerely thought our love would last forever.

I thought the reason Zero never told me he liked me was because we were already so close that we didn't need to say it aloud...

Did this mean everything has been a misunderstanding on my part? The thought made my eyes well up. Hot tears spilled down my face.

"Neigh!"

How dare he make a girl cry? How dare he? How dare he? How dare he?

That night I slipped out of my room and stole away to a small pond deep within the school's campus. We actually weren't allowed out at night, but I knew if I were to remain in my room, I would be forced to attend the matchmaking meeting tomorrow.

I stood on the banks of the pond and peered at my own

image reflected on the still surface of the water.

Well...I certainly look a fine mess right now, I thought and sighed.

My eyes were puffy and bloodshot from crying. My mane that was usually kept so neat and clean was in tangles. Even my coat looked dull and unappealing.

I can't let Zero see me like this, I thought automatically, then immediately shook my head angrily as realization set in.

Oh no, I thought about him again! After I swore I would forget him!

The memory of the afternoon's events came back to me, and my heart started aching again. Tears threatened to fall again.

Stupid Zero! You don't understand my feelings at all, do you?

I broke the surface of the pond with my forelegs and stamped about. But as I gave in to my anger, I felt a presence behind me.

Who's there?!

I whirled around in surprise to find...What was her name

again? Ah, Yuki Cross...

"So it is you, White Lily! What are you doing out here?" she

asked. She looked at me with confused eyes. I turned my head

away from her in a huff.

Leave me alone!

After all, Yuki Cross is my rival. She's the only girl Zero

pays any attention to besides me.

Of all people, I certainly don't want to see your face right now!

I thought at her. But she shamelessly walked right up to stand

beside me.

"I was on patrol when I saw you heading this way," she said.

"But it's way past curfew. We should get you back to the stables."

As if I would go anywhere with her!

Don't you dare touch me!

I shoved her as hard as I could with my nose. She went

tumbling onto the ground.

"Ow..."

Take that, Yuki Cross! And just so you know, I've always had a problem with you. How dare you act so familiar with my beloved Zero? You've even gone as far as living under the same roof with him as though you were family? I'll never forgive you!

"Oof...You're as moody as always, White Lily," she said, standing and brushing dirt off her backside. "Do you not like me? Or do you not want to go home for some reason?"

Both! I thought rebelliously at her. *What is wrong with this girl? Can she not sense how much I loathe her?*

Feeling fed up, I turned my back on her, thinking to go run off somewhere else. But Yuki's next words froze me in my tracks.

"Oh! Could it be you're running away because you don't want to go to the matchmaking meeting tomorrow?"

What? How do you know about that?

"The headmaster told me about it. It's awfully sudden, isn't it?"

Curse that four-eyed meddler! He didn't have to tell her of all people!

Hearing my angry snorts, Yuki continued. "That's it, isn't it? You don't want to go to the matchmaking meeting. That's why you don't want to return to the stables."

"Neigh! Neigh!"

That's right! That's it exactly! So go on ahead and laugh at me! There's nothing more detestable in this world than being laughed at by your rival, but go on. Do it!

I knew she was going to laugh at me. I was sure of it. But oddly, Yuki gave me a sad smile instead.

"I think I understand how you feel, Lily..."

What?

"You hate the idea, don't you? Of course you do—any girl would. How could any girl not hate the thought of marrying someone she doesn't love? If I were in your shoes, I'd probably run away too."

What's this? She seems to understand me more than I thought she would.

For a moment I was tempted to lower my guard with her.

No, no—I can't afford to empathize with this little wretch who clings to Zero!

As though I'd ever open my heart to my rival!

But to be honest, I could sense she didn't have any ill intentions toward me. I decided I could let her stay in my presence for a little while longer.

But just for tonight, I thought at her.

"*Neigh!*"

Now that I'd given permission, Yuki came back over and sat down beside me.

"Lily, you wouldn't happen to already be in love with someone else, would you?" she asked. "If that were the case, a matchmaking meeting would be even worse, wouldn't it?"

Precisely! I thought. *There's no one else for me but Zero!*

"I bet the headmaster doesn't know that you're already in love. Otherwise he wouldn't have agreed to the match."

Probably. I need to give that four-eyes another kick in the pants the next time I see him!

"What's your guy like? I bet he's really cool, isn't he?"

But of course! There is no cooler guy on this entire planet than Zero!

"Neigh!"

At my exclamation, Yuki nodded and chuckled softly. "I see! You must be really proud of your boyfriend. That must be great..." She trailed off, looking downcast. "Compared to you, not only do I not have a boyfriend, I don't even understand boys. Not the teeniest bit!"

Oh, you mean you've felt that way before too? I thought.

She surprised me. Something about Yuki made me warm up to her a bit. It was odd, but I guess even she had a cute side. She was usually running around patrolling the school as a guardian, so I had always assumed she was pretty tough-minded. But I guess even she had the same worries that all girls do.

"I've known Zero for such a long time, but I still can't understand how he thinks," she said pensively. "And Kaname-sama—it's so utterly confusing how or why he would care for

me. Guys are impossible to understand, aren't they? Sometimes they're super-nice, and other times they completely ignore you. I can't follow their feelings at all."

Listening to Yuki, I recalled what Zero had said to me this afternoon.

"Well, you're the right age for a match. You should go for it..."

His words echoed through my head.

When Zero said those words to me earlier, I thought the exact same thing, Yuki, I thought.

"Zero is the worst of all. He always tries to keep his true feelings hidden. I feel like he often doesn't say what he really means. It makes me worry about him so much sometimes..."

Huh? Wait, you don't mean—

Could it be that Zero's words this afternoon had been like that too? Perhaps he hadn't really meant what he'd said? I suddenly felt a ray of light piercing the gloom in my heart.

Could it be that he actually does love me, but only said those things because he thought I'd be happier if I went to the match-

making meeting? Yuki! You're a genius! Thanks to you, maybe I won't have to give up on Zero and hate him forever!

I tapped my nose on Yuki's shoulder to express my gratitude.

"Thank you, Lily. You're trying to encourage me, aren't you?" she said.

Suddenly a voice called out from the woods. "You two! What are you doing out here?"

Zero!

"Zero!" Yuki cried as well.

Zero came running toward us. He seemed a bit frantic and was out of breath. His face was far more expressive than usual.

He's been worried about me! I realized. *He's been looking for me!*

"Yuki, did you bring White Lily out here?" he asked her sternly.

"N-no! I found her after she'd gotten out on her own. It seems she doesn't want to go to the matchmaking meeting tomorrow."

"That's no excuse for you to—"

Don't get upset at her! I thought to him. Before I realized what I was doing, I reached out and chomped down on the top of his head.

He gaped at me. "Why did you bite me?"

B-because you were blaming her! She was only trying to explain why I did it...

Yuki spoke up too. "I'm sure she only did it because she doesn't want to go back. Come on, Zero. Can't we just hide her somewhere for one day?" She had read my mind perfectly.

"Don't be ridiculous," Zero said flatly.

Then it's really true, Zero? You don't care about me?

I could feel my spirits plummet again. Not only did Zero not understand a thing about my feelings, he was talking exclusively to Yuki instead of to me!

"Let's get back. Don't make me worry, dummy." And with that, he reached out and patted Yuki's head.

"Hey! Stop treating me like a kid!" she protested, puffing out her cheeks in mock anger. The way they interacted was so natural and familiar. I felt the blood rush to my head as I watched.

How dare you pat her before you've even patted me? It was just too cruel! And after I'd dared to think I could learn to trust him again!

Farewell, Zero! I truly loved you!

With tears blurring my vision, I turned to run out of the clearing. Zero called out to me.

"Hey! Wait!"

Without meaning to, I obeyed his voice. When the one you love calls out for you to stop, you can't help but do so. That's what it means to have a maiden's heart.

"Don't run away," he said.

But...But...

I wanted to run. I wanted so badly to run, but I couldn't. How long did Zero mean to torment me? Then he said the words.

"I need you in my life," he said. "Let's go home together."
And he gently stroked my cheek.

*Zero...*I realized something. *This means you do really love me?!*

In a flash the world was awash in a rosy glow.

I swear I will love only you for the rest of my life! I declared. With every ounce of emotion I felt, I pressed my nose against his face.

"That was amazing, Zero," Yuki said.

"Not really," he answered. "It's just because I've been taking care of her since she was little. That's why."

Aw, you're acting all shy now, Zero! I thought to him fondly. He really does have such a hard time expressing his true feelings. But to be honest, that's something I love about him too.

"Whatever your faults, I guess you really do take good care of those you care about," Yuki said thoughtfully.

"That's not true," he muttered. "I just wanted to make sure I didn't lose a good place to nap..."

"What? What was that?"

"Nothing."

"White Lily, meet Black Sword!"

Because I'd gone obediently back to my room the previous night, I wound up having to attend the matchmaking meeting after all.

But now that Zero and I have confessed our love, it doesn't matter if I go to this silly meeting or not, I thought.

Black Sword's eyes burned hotly as he looked at me.

You'll make me a fine bride. We should marry immediately—

Certainly not! I interrupted. *No one but Zero will do for me. Who'd want to marry you anyway?*

And with a neigh I bucked up, sending Black Sword flying.

"Ah!"

Immediately after I managed to get in a kick to Headmaster Cross's rear.

Hmph! Take that and get out!

As a result of the incident, all future talk of finding a match for me ended. But I have no regrets about that. I have my Zero. ♡

So today I wander around patiently in my room, waiting for the one I love to come to me. I've arranged the hay to be soft and fluffy, just the way he likes it. I've taken care to make sure I'm completely clean and groomed. Yes, I'm all dressed up for him, so that no matter when he comes, I'll be ready. That's what a true maiden in love does, after all!

Zero, I'm waiting for you. Only for you, my one true love...

Excitement flutters in my chest. I await my beloved and call out to him in my heart.

IN A
THOUSAND
YEARS

Kaito Takamiya strolled up and down the rows of the classroom, observing his students as they bent over their quizzes. When he passed by the window, he paused to glance outside.

I can't believe it's been a year since then.

Outside he could see the damaged main building. Even now signs of the damage inflicted during the battle remained visible on its walls and turrets.

On that day the pureblood vampires had mounted an assault on Cross Academy to bring down Kaname Kuran and his plans to eradicate them. The campus became a battleground where purebloods fought viciously against the vampire hunters trying to protect their final headquarters.

After the battle, the purebloods had slunk back into the darkness, hiding themselves as they recovered. There hadn't been much sign of them lately. Kaito knew this was largely thanks to Kaname Kuran, who sacrificed his heart in order to create anti-vampire weapons for the Hunter Society. That act had increased their power like never before. Kaito found it ironic that it was now, after Kaname was gone, that his influence was stronger than ever.

At least on the surface, life had gone back to normal at Cross Academy. The Hunter Society was another matter altogether. The leadership had broken down and many things remained in limbo—including the rebuilding of Cross Academy.

Even now the "classroom" in which his students were taking a quiz was actually the repurposed dining hall of the staff residence building. In addition to the dining hall, there were a few lecture halls and meeting rooms in the building that were being put to use as classrooms. It would not have been nearly enough to accommodate the original student populace of the school, but after the battle, only a fraction of the student body had returned.

It was for those remaining students that Kaito wished they could rebuild the school as soon as possible. Headmaster Cross and other teachers felt the same way, but the demolition and clearing of the ruined school buildings had barely progressed at all. There was no time frame in place for the completion of the new school.

Further, the number of faculty was decreasing, and many of those who remained were young teachers with little experience like Kaito. This was another challenge Headmaster Cross was dealing with.

Man...I wonder when things will finally settle down again, Kaito thought, unconsciously heaving a deep sigh.

Later that day after classes had ended, a bespectacled boy

stood amid the wreckage of the old school building, examining it critically. "All right, then!" he exclaimed. "Let's get started!" Kasumi Kageyama shoved aside a pile of debris and unearthed a battered desk and chair, then a textbook. He pulled them out one by one and set them reverently aside.

"Even the desks and chairs are in quite a state," Kageyama said sadly as he brushed dirt from the seat of the chair. He heard a voice above him.

"Um, Kageyama?"

Kageyama raised his eyes, adjusted his glasses, and spotted the source of the voice. It belonged to his classmate Sayori Wakaba. She was looking down at him from behind the line of caution tape that cordoned off the wreckage area.

"Ah, Wakaba. Did you need me for something?" he asked.

"I was just on my way back to the dorms when I saw someone out here," said Sayori. "I came to see who it was. But what are you doing down there anyway? Are you looking for something?"

"Not anything in particular," Kageyama answered. "It's just as you see. I'm trying to tidy up a bit."

"All this wreckage?" Sayori asked. She took a good look at their surroundings. There was no possible way a single person could "tidy up" this amount of debris.

"Why are you doing this, Kageyama?" she asked. "Shouldn't it be done by the construction workers?"

"Well, yes, but it's been over a year and they haven't even started clearing this place," he said. "That's why I decided someone has to do something about it!"

"But...do you think you can do it all by yourself?" Sayori asked reasonably. She was right, but Kageyama did not look the least bit dispirited.

"Let me ask you this, Wakaba," he said. "When you see this sight every day, doesn't it make you sad? After what happened, the number of students at this school fell drastically, and the campus isn't lively like it used to be. That's why someone needs to do something, or this situation will never change!"

"Kageyama..."

"Well, I say that, but this is as much as I can do about it right now..." He sighed. "It's at times like these I realize how helpless I really am. If only Kiryu or Yuki Cross were here. Things would be different."

"Yuki..." The moment Sayori spoke her best friend's name, a deep ache filled her chest. Yuki was gone now. There were days when Sayori thought about how she would likely never again share just one more day at this school with her best friend. It saddened her.

Before Sayori knew what she was doing, she crossed the caution tape line to help Kageyama.

"Wakaba?" he said in surprise.

"I'm going to help return this school to how it was when Yuki and the others were here too. I feel the same way about it that you do, Kageyama." As she spoke, Kaito appeared.

"You two, what do you think you're doing?" he asked. "It's dangerous in there."

As a dyed-in-the-wool honor student, Kageyama could not help but immediately bow politely to the teacher that was giving them a "get out of there right now" glare. Ignoring it, he said, "Mr. Takamiya! I want to return this school to its former glory!"

"Yes, but there's no reason you two need to be down there doing the clearing."

"But we don't want to see our school in this broken-down state anymore! If we can help get the school rebuilt faster, maybe more students will come back!"

As Kageyama made his passionate speech, the light of the setting sun glinted off his glasses, making him appear almost heroic. Sayori nodded emphatically to add her support. Looking at the two of them, Kaito couldn't help but rub his forehead in exasperation.

"I understand how you guys feel, but right now the school is dealing with plenty of issues that are delaying the construction," he said.

"What sort of issues, sir?" Kageyama asked. "Perhaps I can

be of help resolving them? I'd do anything to return our school

to its former glory—"

Kageyama was cut off as the patch of dirt he stood on sud-

denly gave way. He plummeted straight out of sight.

"Kageyama?!" Sayori cried.

"Hold on, Wakaba, don't move!" warned Kaito. "The ground

is unstable."

He quickly stepped over the line of caution tape and hurried

to the spot Kageyama had disappeared, peering down through

the new hole in the hillside of debris.

They heard Kageyama's voice from below. "Whoa! What

is this?"

"Are you okay down there?" Kaito called. "You're darn lucky!

Hey! What are you doing?" It was a miracle Kageyama hadn't

been injured by the fall. He now stood at the bottom of the hole

waving excitedly up at his teacher.

"I've made a huge discovery!" he cried. "There's buried

treasure down here!"

What Kageyama had found was a bona fide treasure chest that looked like it had come straight out of a children's storybook. Between the two of them they were able to dig out the half-buried chest and carry it back up to the surface.

"I can't believe something like this was down there!" Sayori exclaimed, gazing at it in fascination. Kaito broke the lock with his shovel and the three gathered around, brushing dirt off the lid and then pushing it open.

"Huh? This is..."

Kageyama was the first to peer inside, his glasses flashing. Inside the chest was a graduation album, journals, letters written by students to their future selves, scenic photos, and what appeared to be preserved corsages and neckties worn to the school ball.

"It seems to be full of commemorative items from a school graduation," Kageyama said.

"Ah, a time capsule, huh?" Kaito said.

"Oh! I think this belonged to the headmaster!" Sayori

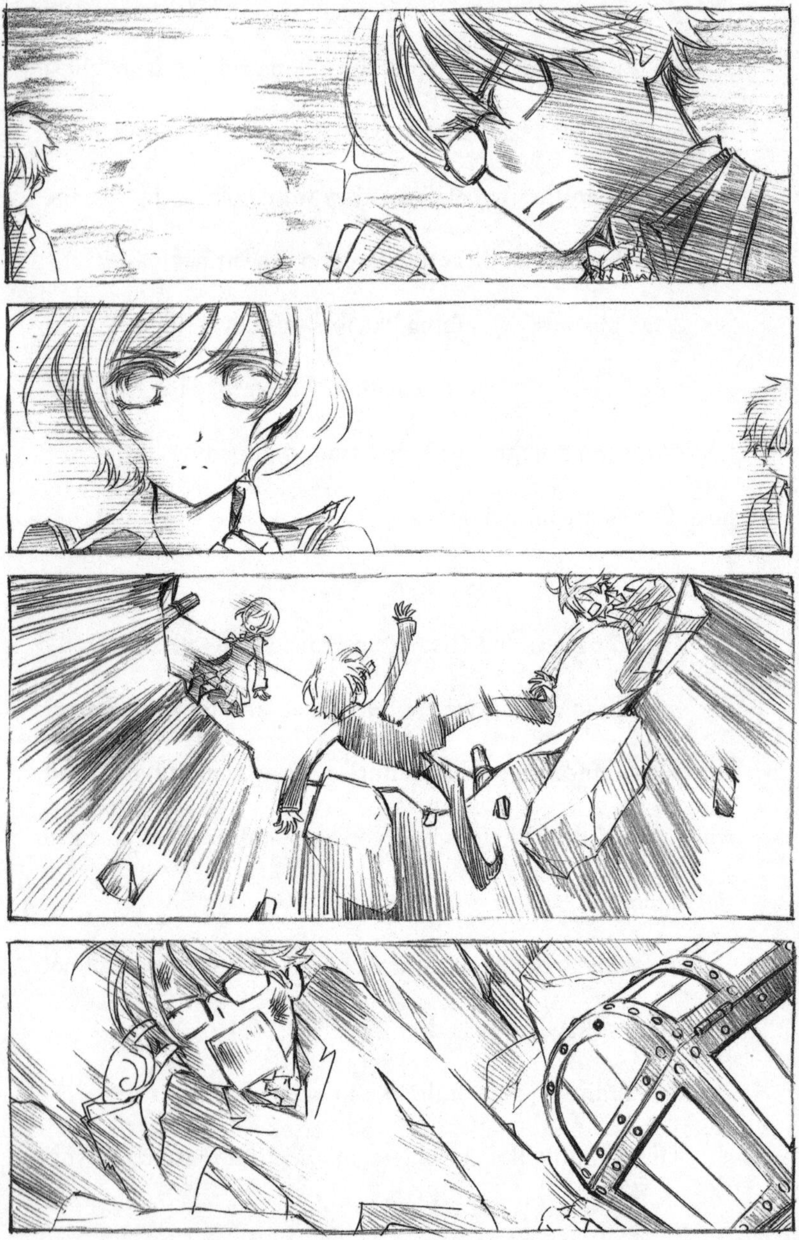

exclaimed, holding out a menu signboard she had picked up. On it were the names of various foods written by hand. It must have been used for that year's ball.

"My Style Ballsy Sashimi, My Style Ballsy Fish with Soy Sauce, My Style Ballsy Tempura...What the heck? Was he trying to get cute by making everything into little balls and calling it 'ballsy'? That is completely unappetizing..." Kaito muttered, making a face. Kageyama, who had been poking around in the chest's contents, suddenly gave a small cry.

"Hey! Take a look at this!" He whipped out a thin notebook and flipped it open to show his companions. Rows of neat writing outlined the plans for an event, supplemented by hand-drawn maps of various venues.

"This is perfect!" Kageyama exclaimed. "These plans are just what we need to rebuild our school and bring back everyone's smiles!"

A few weeks after the time capsule had been discovered, all the students at the academy were summoned to a meeting in the dining hall of the former staff residence. Several desks had been pushed together in the center of the room to form a sort of platform, upon which sat a heavy-looking treasure chest wrapped in chains.

"What's this about afternoon classes being canceled?" a student asked.

"What's with that box?" said another.

No one seemed to know why they had been gathered there. The students glanced quizzically around at one another. Standing against the back wall of the room, Akatsuki Kain and Ruka Souen were also present.

"We came all this way to check up on the school, but I'm surprised how few students are left," Kain commented.

"I wonder what's going on here," Ruka wondered aloud. "Where are Shiki and Rima? They're the ones who told us to come here. So where are they?"

The pair of aristocrats stood out as usual. Various students snuck peeks at them over their shoulders.

"That guy is really cute, isn't he?"

"The girl next to him is insanely pretty!"

"I wonder if they are graduates of the Night Class."

A Night Class still existed at the academy, but the memories of Kain's generation had been erased from most of the students' minds. As a result, the presence of the beautiful pair was attracting a good deal of attention.

"Maybe we should just leave," Ruka murmured.

"Aw, don't say that. We haven't been here in ages!"

"Oh! Those girls..."

Ruka spotted a group of girls clad in the familiar white uniforms of the Night Class. They had an elite air about them that was unique to vampires. With the sun still up, very few Night Class students had come to the assembly, so those who did stood out all the more.

"They must have been part of Sara Shirabuki's flock," Kain

guessed. "They seem to be carrying on pretty well without her."

One of the Night Class students broke away from the rest and shyly approached the pair.

"It's lovely to see you again, Kain, Ruka," she said.

"You're Maria Kurenai, aren't you?" said Kain.

"You stayed on in the Night Class?" asked Ruka.

She nodded. "Yes, I did. I was a bit torn about it for a while, but in the end...Well, anyway, it is very nice seeing you again."

With a small bob of her head to mark the end of her formal greeting, Maria went to rejoin her friends, who were part of a different group of students than those who had been devoted to Sara. From the easy, familiar way Maria and her friends laughed and spoke together, it seemed she had managed to achieve a peaceful school life for herself. The thought brought both relief and a bit of envy to Ruka.

"Do you get the sense that the atmosphere is a bit different from when we were at school here? It seems more fun somehow," she murmured.

"Yeah. But when we were students, we weren't exactly here to have a fun, carefree time," said Kain.

The bell indicating the start of afternoon classes rang. Using it as his signal to begin, Kageyama climbed up onto the makeshift platform and stepped in front of the microphone that had been set up there. "Ladies and gentlemen! Thank you very much for coming today," he began. "Not long ago, Wakaba, Mr. Takamiya, and I unearthed something extraordinary near the old school building—this treasure chest! Within it lay many sleeping treasures, one of which was this notebook!" Kageyama held up the notebook in question so that everyone could see it. "Within this notebook is written the notes and plans for a certain special event. Today we'd like to recreate that event here! This event will be called 'The Cross Academy Treasure Hunt,' and it starts now!"

Though Kageyama's breathless delivery of this news had been excitement itself, the response from the students was flat.

"Oh, a school event? I thought something big was

happening..."

"They seriously canceled classes for this?"

"A treasure hunt? That sounds sketchy to me..."

Kageyama looked a tad crushed at his fellow students' lack of enthusiasm, but he quickly pulled himself together and again raised the microphone to his mouth.

"Now then, I shall explain the rules! Wakaba, if you would kindly come up?"

Sayori stepped up onto the platform and unfolded a very large sheet of paper she was holding. On it they had written a simple version of the rules:

1) At Station 1 (this room), collect the first clue.

2) Follow the clue's instructions to get to Station 2.

3) At Station 2, clear the required mission and receive the next clue.

"You will continue on in that way until you've cleared all the missions," Kageyama explained. "The first one to finish them all and return here will receive the treasure! However, you should note that everyone's routes will not be the same, and that the treasure hunt has a time limit. It's over when the end-of-the-day bell rings. Everyone, please do your best!"

Kageyama raised a whistle to his lips and let out a shrill blast signaling the start of the hunt, and Sayori pulled the cord to split open the paper orb hanging suspended from the ceiling. Pieces of folded paper came showering down on the crowd.

"You can pick whichever clue you want," Kageyama explained. "Just one per person, please! Follow the instructions in the note to get started."

The students began reaching down to select a folded piece of paper, opening them up to read the clues inside.

"Huh? What's this?"

"A demon? Say what?!"

"Mine says, 'Have a quiz show battle with a school celebrity'!"

"Cool. That actually sounds kind of fun!"

"Hey, are all of you guys going to do this?"

The students warmed up to the idea and began chattering

among themselves.

"What simpletons," Ruka muttered, turning her head away from the spectacle, only to find that Kain had picked up one of the notes and was examining it.

"W-what are you doing picking that up?" she demanded.

"It says to defeat the demon in the Sun Dormitory," Kain replied.

"Wait...You're not seriously planning to do this?"

"It is a special school event, after all. Would it be so bad to participate? We did come out here to see how Cross Academy was getting on. This will give us a chance to look all over the campus."

So Kain and Ruka, following their clue, wound up at the Sun Dormitory. Thanks to its distance from the main campus, the building was still intact and looked exactly as it had in the past.

The clue had come with some fine print: "Warning: The demon is in the Boys Dorm. Don't use this as an excuse to sneak into the Girls Dorm!" So it was to the Boys Dorm that the pair turned their steps.

"It's dark in here..." Kain said.

It was pitch black inside the dorm. All the lights had been turned off for the treasure hunt, and the windows were covered with blackout blinds. There was but one source of illumination on the entire floor—a single candle, flickering atmospherically at the end of a long hallway.

"I guess we head that way?" said Kain.

Darkness was hardly something that would scare a pair of vampires, but they did encounter something odd.

"Ow!" cried a voice in the darkness. Kain and Ruka realized that a student was lying on the floor at their feet.

"Ugh," the student groaned. "It's impossible...to beat him..." And with that, the boy passed out.

"Hey! Are you okay?" Kain cried, shaking him.

"What is going on here?" Ruka wondered. She turned to stare down the hallway, her brow furrowed. Now that she was looking closely, she could see the hallway was littered with the collapsed forms of a large number of people. Though the students were likely just dazed or unconscious, the scene looked like the piles of bodies that would be found on a particularly violent battlefield.

"It seems like a fairly troublesome demon has taken up residence here," Kain commented. Squaring his shoulders, he led Ruka into the hallway. When they reached the candle, they found an entranceway to a room. Above the entrance was a doorplate that read "Dormitory President." Apparently the president of the Sun Dormitory had given up his room for the treasure hunt.

The moment Kain and Ruka stepped into the room, a voice came reverberating out of the darkness.

"It looks like some worthy opponents have finally come..."

Squinting their eyes, the pair found themselves facing none other than Toga Yagari, clad entirely in sleek black clothing. Draped over his broad shoulders was a grand cape. Upon his head he wore a hairband from which a pair of fake horns protruded. He looked utterly ridic—that is, mysterious.

"Well, well," he said in his booming voice. "I wasn't expecting the fair Lady Souen to show up today! This is a glamorous party indeed."

Though Yagari had said all of this quite solemnly, it was impossible for Ruka to take him seriously in that getup. "Really, how can you bear to dress yourself in that foolish manner?" she demanded. "Aren't you embarrassed?"

"You see," Yagari began, glancing away sheepishly, "there is a good reason for this—"

Just then a bright flash filled the room with light.

"What was that?" Ruka cried, turning to find Kaito standing in the doorway with a camera in his hands.

"Yagari, you look absolutely stunning in that," he said with a chuckle.

"K-Kaito!" Yagari cried. "This is all your fault!"

"My fault? You lost to me fair and square at rock-paper-scissors, so don't go blaming me for this. We decided beforehand that it would be a one-round, sudden-death game. The winner would get to be the cameraman while the loser had to play the demon of the dorm, remember?"

"That may be so, but I...I'm your master! How could you make the man who taught you everything you know wear *this*?!"

"In a battle of fortune, the student may easily surpass the teacher," Kaito intoned. "And anyway, I really didn't want to be caught dead in that costume..."

"Why, you—"

"This is ridiculous," Ruka said. "Akatsuki, we're leaving!" Ruka turned on her heel to walk away.

"Hold on just a minute, now!" Yagari called out behind her. "Unfortunately anyone who steps into this room must do battle with me. It says on your clue that you're supposed to defeat the demon, right? Well, I'm your demon!"

Kain's expression sharpened at his words. "I was the one who picked that clue. If you want a fight, it'll be with me."

"Oh ho! Pretty sure of yourself, aren't you? But didn't you lose a fight against Zero in the past?" Yagari asked. He had already chalked up the battle as an easy win. He continued to smile congenially.

"You're bringing that up?" Kain's battle lust activated instantly.

Yagari shrugged lightly in response. "Come at me! That's what I'd like to say. Too bad the battle we're supposed to have isn't like what you're thinking. It's a battle of these kind of arms." Yagari grinned and flexed one of his bulging biceps. "It's a battle to see who can do more push-ups!"

The rules were simple. Within the allotted three minutes, the person who could complete more push-ups would be the winner. The students in the hallway had collapsed of exhaustion long before the three minutes were up. Those who had managed to last the full three minutes had still been unable to match Yagari's speed and push-up count. He was yet undefeated.

After hearing the rules, Ruka wasn't impressed. "Utterly

ridiculous!" she muttered.

"Well, you can run away if you really want to," Yagari said. "I'll just remain undefeated, I suppose. Go ahead and acknowledge your defeat and leave now if you like."

Ruka flashed him a glare. "Akatsuki," she said, "accept his challenge."

"As you wish," Kain said with a mock bow. He turned to Yagari. "It looks like I've received my princess's permission to take you down."

Yagari and Kain got into push-up position on the designated mat. Kaito, acting as timekeeper, watched the second hand of his wristwatch until it reached the top.

"Start!" he yelled.

Without anyone noticing, the doorway had filled up with students curiously watching the match.

"Th-that's amazing!"

"He's actually able to keep up with Mr. Yagari!"

In the midst of the clamor, Yagari and Kain kept up

their rapid pace, showing no signs of tiring. Kain picked up his pace slightly, having no intention of losing to his former ethics lecturer.

This guy's not too bad, Yagari thought.

That's the impressive power of a top vampire hunter, all right, Kain thought. *He won't go down easily.*

Though push-ups are a basic exercise everyone knows how to do, they aren't easy. They require the upper half of one's body to support one's entire weight while engaging in a repetitive up-and-down motion. Doing them in long sets takes a toll on the arms. The competitor's rapid, steady pace was proof that both men had substantial upper body strength.

You're definitely the first challenger with this much game, Yagari thought.

Yeah, you're not so bad yourself, Kain thought.

The two communicated these sentiments silently with a meeting of glances. The mutual acknowledgement was not lost on either Ruka or Kaito as they kept vigilant watch over the battle.

"What is happening between those two?" Ruka murmured.

"They're the type to get fired up over stuff like this," Kaito replied.

The match ended with both competitors having completed exactly the same number of push-ups. It was a draw. Though neither had managed to crush the other as promised, both Yagari and Kain looked refreshed and satisfied.

"It was a good match," said Yagari. "But since you didn't technically beat me, I can't hand over the clue for the next station."

"I'm good," Kain said. "This was enough for me. And anyway, if I tried to complete any more missions, I'm pretty sure it would only irritate my princess."

Oddly enough it seemed the seeds of friendship had somehow been planted between the two during their match. Kain gave Yagari a wide smile before waving and heading out the exit after Ruka. After they had exited the Sun Dormitory,

Ruka halted suddenly and turned to face Kain with an arch look.

"You could have stayed and challenged him again until you won, you know."

"Nah, it's fine," said Kain. "According to the rules, you get only one shot per mission. I'd rather go see how Hanabusa is doing. You know how gets. He needs encouragement from time to time."

"True..."

Aido was currently spending his days buried in his research. Using a certain journal he'd found in the library of the Kuran residence as his basis, he was attempting to perfect a "medicine" that could turn vampires human. But in order to complete it, he required technology that did not yet exist, so Aido was working on inventing that technology himself. As he'd only just begun this work, there were many long hours of trial and error ahead of him. He had been keeping his friends informed of his progress through letters.

"He said he's been renting out equipment from the academy for use in experiments," said Kain. "Shall we head over?"

Ruka was silent for a moment. With a slight frown she murmured, "Will the day truly come when Kaname-sama wakes again?"

"It will. I'm sure of it," Kain said gently. He gave Ruka's shoulder a soft pat and began walking.

The inside of the classroom had been made up to resemble the set of a quiz show. Two chairs for contestants sat in the middle, and in one of those chairs was Senri Shiki.

"Look! Look! It's that model, Shiki!"

"No way! Rima Toya is here too!"

The excited chatter of the onlookers—the "studio audience"—rippled through the room as the quiz show proceeded. The rules of the show were that two contestants competed to answer three trivia questions. The one who had two correct answers was the winner. Rima, for some reason, was serving as the host of the show.

"Next contestant, please," she intoned.

"C-coming!"

Clutching her clue in her hand, a female student came up to the front of the room and sat down in the seat beside Shiki.

"M-my name is Sena Mikimoto!" she said nervously. "I-I'm such a big fan of yours, S-Senri!"

"...Thanks," said Shiki. "Do your best."

"I-I will!" Mikimoto squeaked.

However, she decidedly did not do her best. All she did was stare at Shiki's profile for the entire round of competition.

"...Better luck next time," said Shiki.

"Thanks," said Mikimoto. "But I got to look at your face from so close up that I really couldn't be happier!" She stood from her seat and was greeted by a polite round of applause from the audience as she made her way back among them.

"Now," Rima continued in her usual monotone, "next contestant, please."

"That's me!" cried another girl, coming forward. "I'm Maya Takizawa, and I'm a fan of Rima!"

"Thank you," said Rima. Her expression remained the same whether she was speaking her thanks or reading quiz questions. "Next we have a fan service question: What shape are the frames of the headmaster's glasses?"

"Huh? The headmaster?" said Maya. "D-darn. I have no interest in him, so I have no idea!" As Maya grasped her temples in concentration, Shiki pressed the buzzer in front of him to answer the question.

"He usually wears oval-shaped frames for his regular glasses, but occasionally he wears sunglasses with star-shaped frames," said Shiki.

"Correct," said Rima.

"W-wait a sec," said Maya. "How on earth do you know that?"

"It's part of being a model," said Shiki. "If I see something once, I tend to remember it."

Shiki proceeded to defeat one girl after the next in this manner. It went much the same with his male challengers as well.

"This question involves the Cross Academy school uniform," read Rima. "The uniform's shirt is true white and the necktie is cardinal red. So what color is the trim over the toe area of the socks in the standard girls' uniform?"

"What the?! Wait a second!" cried the male student currently challenging Shiki. As he sputtered in protest at the question, Shiki buzzed in.

"Black."

"Correct. Incidentally, the school-approved shoe color is sepia."

"Dang it!" cried the challenger. "The answer was so obvious I freaked out for nothing!" He chewed his lip in frustration.

With Shiki's buzzing in with correct answers, his winning streak seemed to have no end in sight.

"All the questions are so easy too..."

"Shiki, why don't you go a little easier on them?"

"Don't want to. Headmaster Cross said that if I win every match, he'll give me a year's supply of Pokkin Choco."

"Why don't you just buy it yourself? Now then, next contestant, please."

As Shiki and Rima continued to cut through the pack of challengers, Headmaster Cross eventually poked his head into the room to see how things were proceeding.

"Oh! It looks like they're really enjoying themselves!" he said happily. "Just look at how fired up they are!"

"Huh? They look pretty blasé about the whole thing to me," said Kaito, who had followed Headmaster Cross in to take photos of the event.

"I'm so glad I decided to put them in charge of running the quiz show challenge," Headmaster Cross continued. "They're very popular with the students, so I'm sure everyone is glad to have this chance to have fun together!"

As Kaito watched Shiki speed-buzz and crush his current opponent, he couldn't help but feel there was more frustration in the room than fun.

"But with things as they are, is anyone going to be able to complete this treasure hunt?" Kaito asked.

"Of course!" Headmaster Cross declared. "I have a plan to ensure that someone makes it to the end!"

"But how?" asked Kaito. "Between Yagari and these two, it seems pretty impossible to me."

Headmaster Cross shook his head and wagged a knowing finger at him. "You just don't understand, Kaito," he said. "If their opponents weren't so demonically powerful, the students wouldn't get nearly as fired up as they are!"

"I guess..." Kaito managed to agree weakly.

One of the students in the studio audience turned around and spotted the headmaster. "Headmaster Cross is here!" he exclaimed.

"Hey, he really does wear oval-shaped glasses!"

"Quick, someone check his shirt color! And what color are his socks?"

Headmaster Cross suddenly found himself surrounded by students. "I'm, um, not too sure what's happening, but I think it's time I was on my way!" he cried. "Kaito, continue to take excellent commemorative photos of today's event, okay?" And with that, Headmaster Cross fled.

"Sure thing, Headmaster Cross," Kaito called as several students took off running after their departing prey. He watched them for another moment before turning back to the event at hand. Several students were staring at him now.

"Mr. Takamiya, what color are your socks?" asked one.

"Can we measure how big your hands are? It seems like the sort of question that would come up in this quiz," said another.

"Huh?" said Kaito. "Um, I'm not sure what you all are—"

Maybe I'd better go too. Kaito whirled on his heel and took flight.

Kasumi Kageyama arrived at the grand hall where the

school ball had once been held. The room was not currently in use. A section of it had been completely destroyed during the battle at Cross Academy. It was not one of the stations for today's treasure hunt, but fearing that students might have come to it by mistake, Kageyama decided to stop by to check on it during his station rounds.

How nostalgic, he thought. He reached up to push open the grand set of doors that led into the main ballroom and stepped softly inside. He was surprised to find that someone else was there too. Standing in the middle of the ballroom and gazing around was a bespectacled girl who wore her hair in two braids. When she turned and saw Kageyama, her face warmed into a nostalgic smile.

"It's you, Kageyama..."

"Shindo! It's been so long!" Kageyama exclaimed. Nadeshiko Shindo was one of the students who had not immediately returned to Cross Academy after its partial destruction. It had been a while since he'd last seen her.

"Today is my first day back at school," she told him.

"I see! It's so fantastic to see you again!" Kageyama said, smiling.

"You look well, Kageyama. It seems you're not only the class representative now, but also the president of the boys dormitory? Maya mentioned it in a letter she sent me."

"Oh, Takizawa? That's right, you two were roommates in the Girls Dorm, weren't you?" asked Kageyama.

Nadeshiko laughed. "You have a good memory."

"My memory is the one thing I do have a bit of confidence in." Kageyama said. The two stood comfortably together, smiling as they spoke. They had been in the same class since middle school, so even though they hadn't met in a while, there was no awkwardness between them.

"So what are you doing out here?" asked Kageyama. "Aren't you participating in the treasure hunt?"

"I am," said Nadeshiko, "but on my way to a station, I saw the Grand Hall. I felt so nostalgic that I had to come see it again."

"I see." Kageyama gazed around the ballroom, recalling memories. "During our first year, my class was in charge of setting up the school ball. We did such a good job that I believe it went down in Cross Academy history."

"True. But if I recall," Nadeshiko teased, "you guys got the job because your test score average was the lowest of all the classes."

"Wah! Don't mention that! Just remembering that shame puts a bad feeling in my chest! It was all because of Yuki Cross and Kiryu!" Kageyama gripped his head comically in grief.

Nadeshiko, however, stopped smiling.

Kiryu...

On that night it had taken every shred of courage she possessed to ask him to dance with her.

"I'm busy," he had said as he turned her down. It had hurt at the time, but now she found she could look back on it without heartache.

Huh? Wait a moment—why does it feel like I'm forgetting something important about Kiryu? Nadeshiko wondered. When she tried to think hard and remember, it felt like a fog obscured her mind.

"What's the matter, Shindo?" asked Kageyama.

"Huh? Oh, nothing." She quickly changed the subject. "S-so, how is Kiryu now?"

"Hm? Well, he's sometimes here, sometimes not. Just like always, he comes and goes and cuts classes as he pleases."

"I see..." Nadeshiko said, smiling softly.

I believe Shindo had her memories of the Night Class being vampires erased, Kageyama thought to himself. The same had been done to him as well, though after reuniting with Ruka one day in his second year, he had abruptly remembered the truth. Not all of it, he knew, but a good deal.

He was aware Ruka was at the academy today. But at her side had stood Akatsuki Kain, looking as though he belonged there. It was frustrating to admit, of course, but he felt that there was no other man more suited to Ruka.

Ruka looked so beautiful on the night of the ball, he thought. She had worn a royal blue dress that night and looked more elegant than any other girl in the room. She had been like a glorious flower in full, radiant bloom that night. The memory of her in that dress was one of Kageyama's greatest treasures.

"I wish we could hold a ball here again," Kageyama murmured.

"Me too," Nadeshiko agreed. "I would love to attend another one."

"Okay, then—leave it to me! I'll make it my new project to get the ball reinstated!"

Fired up, Kageyama clenched his right hand into a fist and pumped it passionately up at the patches of sky peeking through the crumbling walls.

After we fix the main school building, I'll ask Headmaster Cross if we can rebuild this hall next!

In the subterranean levels of the academy, there was a certain door that did not open. In front of this door Takuma Ichijo kept vigil. Standing in quiet repose with his eyes closed, he looked very much like a knight standing guard over his slumbering king. The chamber lay silent, and nothing within it stirred but the barest of underground drafts.

Into this silent sanctuary came a burst of lively voices, echoing from the stairwell.

"What? There's a place like this at Cross Academy?" asked one.

"What should we do?" asked another. "We must've taken a wrong turn somewhere!"

A group of students had accidentally found their way into this isolated place while attempting to follow their treasure hunt clues.

A kind smile warming his face, Ichijo opened his eyes and called out to them. "Hello there. Were you looking for something?"

"Oh!" said one of the girls. "S-sorry. We were just looking for the underground storeroom..."

"A storeroom?" Ichijo echoed. "Oh, the one where the old teaching guides are kept?"

"Yes, I think so. Do you know where it is?"

"Let's see..." Takuma glanced over the map the girls held out to him and pointed out the route they needed to take.

"Thank you so much. We're so sorry to bother you again," said another of the girls, "but, sir...I don't think we've seen you before. Are you a new teacher by any chance?"

"Oh, no, no," said Ichijo quickly. "I'm...just someone connected to Cross Academy."

"Oh really? Then we'll have to come back here again sometime and thank you properly for your help!"

Despite their earnest request, Ichijo shook his head apologetically.

"I'm afraid you mustn't come here again," he said. "There

are rumors, you know, that ghosts haunt this place..."

"Eek! You shouldn't joke about things like—"

Before the girl could finish speaking, Ichijo vanished from before their eyes.

"Huh?!"

"C-could it be that he was a..."

All the color drained from the girls' faces.

"L-let's get out of here!" they cried and ran from the room.

After their footsteps had faded, Ichijo stepped back out from behind the pillar he had hidden behind, chuckling softly to himself.

"I might have scared them a bit too much with that," he said to himself. "But they really shouldn't come near this place."

Ichijo looked up at the closed door and thought about the man who slumbered behind it. He who had wished for the end of vampires for so long that he had ultimately hurled his heart into a raging furnace to aid such a future. And he was Ichijo's best friend.

Kaname...

"Ichijo-sama, why not participate in this treasure hunt event?" came a voice nearby. "It's a rare opportunity that shouldn't be missed. I will stand guard here in your place."

When Ichijo turned toward the voice, Seiren appeared beside him. "Forgive me, I did not mean to startle you," she said. "I only thought you should take the chance to breathe some fresh air."

"How about yourself?" Ichijo asked. "Are you done with whatever it was you were helping Aido with?"

"Yes," Seiren replied. "There is nothing else he needs me to do today. So please feel free..."

"I'm fine. This is the role I've chosen. I'm here because I truly want to be." After he'd spoken, Ichijo paused as though to reconsider his answer and pretended to have a change of heart. "But I suppose you're right. It wouldn't be bad to breathe some fresh air now and then."

"Then please leave this to me," said Seiren.

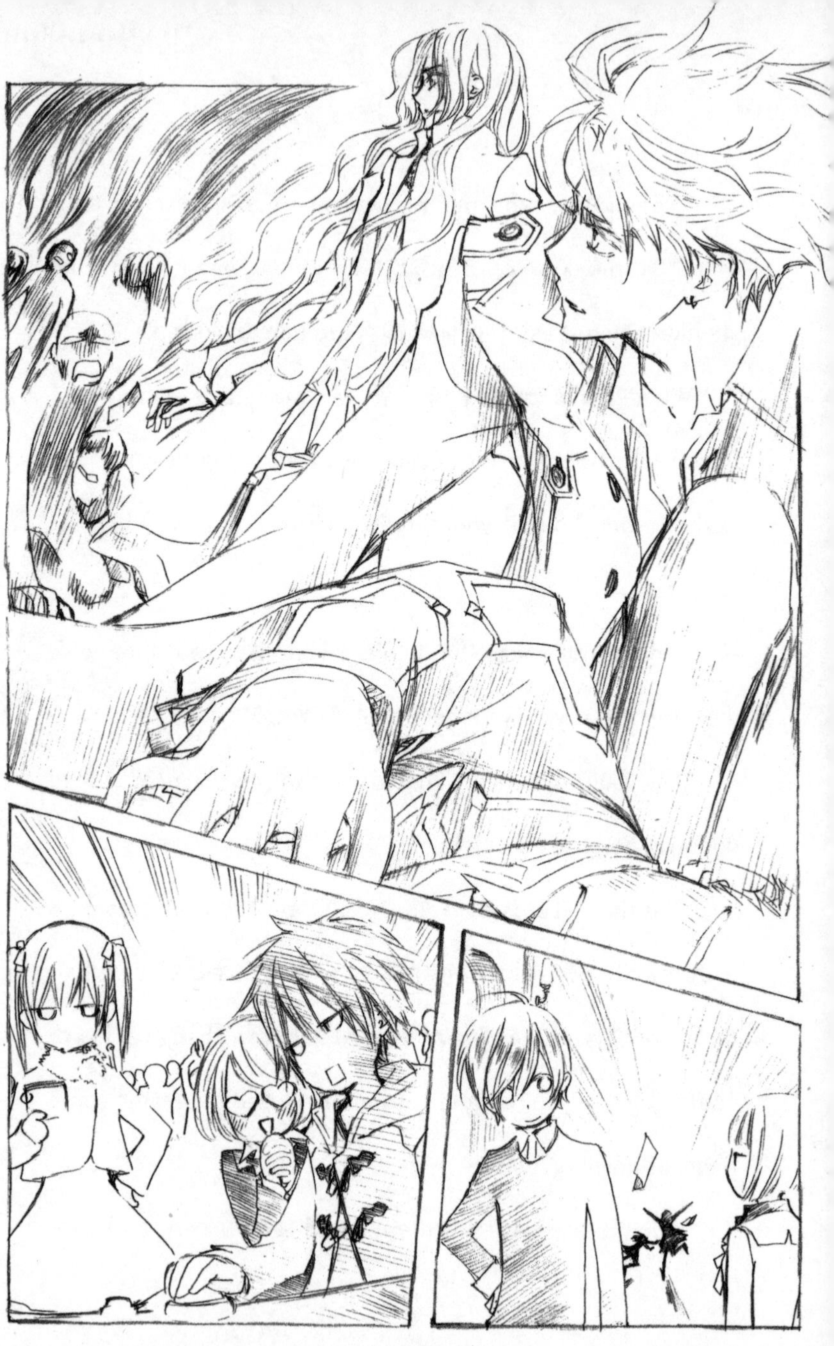

"All right," Ichijo agreed. "I'll step out for a bit."

Smiling cheerfully, Ichijo stepped away from the door and made his way out of the underground passageway.

Once in a while I ought to give her a chance to be alone with Kaname too, he thought.

As an event organizer, Sayori was also making rounds to all the treasure hunt stations. Her next stop was the stables.

Please don't let anyone have been injured, she prayed.

It seemed obvious that involving White Lily—Cross Academy's infamously foul-tempered "wild horse"—in the treasure hunt was an extremely bad idea. But Headmaster Cross had dismissed her fears.

"It'll be fine!" he had declared and was so keen on the idea of using the stables as one of the mission stations that she and Kageyama had no other choice but to relent.

Sayori approached the building with considerable trepidation. As she came near the entrance, she began to hear the telltale screams.

Oh no...

The scene inside was just as she had imagined. Piles of battered students were strewn everywhere.

"My sore butt..."

"White Lily is a terror!"

White Lily was standing by a pile of hay, pawing it imperiously with her foreleg.

"My poor bed! I always keep it neat and fluffed up just the way Zero likes it so he can nap on it whenever he comes! How dare you lowly peasants mess it up?!"

Though Sayori was unable to hear the horse's thoughts, she did understand that White Lily was in a very foul mood. "She sure is angry," she murmured. It was just what she had predicted—just what anyone would have predicted. Sayori gave a bitter laugh.

As she stood there, the bruised youths lying on the floor of the stable began calling out to her in mournful voices.

"Wakaba, this is the end of the line for us..."

"Who decided to have this horrible mission anyway?"

Sayori flinched. "Well, um..." she began, when a familiar voice interrupted her.

"What a racket," Zero said irritably as he strode into the stable. He stopped and glanced around.

"Why are there so many people in here?" he asked. "I thought classes were canceled this afternoon."

"One of the missions for the treasure hunt takes place here," one of the boys explained. "Right over there, in fact." He pointed to the wall behind White Lily. Several white envelopes sat atop the wall. It seemed not a single person had managed to take one so far.

"What are those doing there?" Zero asked, starting to look annoyed again.

"W-well, that's where Headmaster Cross suggested we put them..." Sayori answered.

White Lily let out an angry whinny and kicked out imperiously with her back legs at that. *"Why that four-eyed meddler!"* White Lily raged internally. *"Next time I see him, I'll kick his rear a hundred times and then send him flying!"*

No one could hear Lily's rant, but they knew the horse's fury had somehow doubled. The students shrank back in fear.

"That idiot headmaster," Zero muttered. "He really never does anything right, does he? Guess I've got no choice..." He began stroking Lily's mane. Lily's entire manner changed immediately. Now she was docile without a trace of wildness in her.

"Tee hee! Well, I'll never say no to having Zero beside me..."

"White Lily has calmed down!" cried one of the boys.

"You're amazing, Kiryu!" said another.

The boys took the chance to make a mad rush for the envelopes on the wall. Once procured, the students dashed away. Lily gaped at the trampled hay in their wake.

"M-my bed!"

Lily was about to lose her temper again, but Zero said, "I'll change the hay for you after this, okay? Just be good."

"*Oh, okay then,*" Lily seemed to agree, and stood still.

Having witnessed Lily's complete transformation under Zero's influence, Sayori said admiringly, "You know, Zero, you're really a nice guy too, aren't you?"

"Huh? Not really. I just wanted to come take a nap here, that's all." As though to prove his point, Zero plopped down onto the hay at Lily's feet and rolled onto his side.

"I guess I'll continue my rounds of the treasure hunt stations," Sayori said as she started to leave. Pausing a moment, she asked, "Um...has Yuki written to you or anything?"

"..."

Zero made no reply and remained with his back turned to her.

At last the final bell rang, signaling the end of the treasure hunt. The students streamed back into the dining hall. Several faces looked utterly exhausted, but most of the students were talking excitedly with friends, exchanging tales of their various adventures during the afternoon.

Kageyama made his way up onto the makeshift stage once again and looked at his fellow students.

"Welcome back, everyone! Well done!" he began. "Did you have fun on your treasure hunt?"

"My arms are still sore..."

"I-I'm...*achoo!*"

"I got to sit beside Shiki! I was so happy!"

Various responses filled the room. Finally Kageyama cleared his throat, and the room fell quiet again.

"We had push-ups, arm wrestling, handstands, spicy curry bread-eating, yarn-rolling, hot pepper-consuming, quiz shows, and manga trivia...There were a variety of missions here today. But I do believe the White Lily trap was the toughest one to overcome?"

"I only made it to the push-up contest!" cried one of the boys, causing a general murmur to stir through the crowd.

Then it was time to name the winner of the treasure hunt.

"Now then," said Kageyama, "I will announce the name of the person who managed to complete all the missions and win the treasure! The winner is the former vice president of the Night Class, Takuma Ichijo!"

Kain, Ruka, Shiki, and Rima, who were all standing off by themselves in a corner of the room, looked to the stage in surprise.

"Takuma!" Ruka said in mild exasperation. "When on earth did he come out to join the hunt?"

"Ichijo won..." murmured Shiki.

"That's kind of amazing," said Rima.

"I bet our former vice president won by dominating the manga trivia contest," said Kain.

The four exchanged a knowing look. Ichijo's passion for manga was a mighty thing. He was often so engrossed in his manga that he continued reading well into the day.

Kageyama continued his speech. "As promised, we shall now award Ichijo with the contents of the treasure chest! Please go ahead and open it."

The chains had been removed from the treasure chest. Ichijo approached it. "Thank you very much," he said. "Here I go!" Ichijo lifted the lid of the chest up while the students watched curiously.

"What's inside?" someone asked.

"Well, it's a treasure chest, so it better have some awesome treasure inside!"

"Is it full of gold and silver and jewels?"

As the students waited in anticipation, Yagari and Kaito stood against the wall opposite the elite vampires and turned to Sayori, who was next to them. "Hey, is there really treasure in the treasure chest?" asked Kaito.

"Well," replied Sayori, "Headmaster Cross insisted that he select the prize. He refused to tell Kageyama and me what it was."

"So no one knows what's inside..." Yagari mused. "That worries me. If he put something stupid in there, I think I may seriously have to go punch him. Making me dress up in that ridiculous costume...Ugh! Just remembering it makes my skin crawl."

Yagari was back in his own clothing now, looking no worse for wear despite the hundreds of push-ups he had done that afternoon.

They're both much tougher than they look, Sayori thought.

Ichijo was peeking inside at the contents of the treasure chest.

"Ichijo! Reach in and grab your prize!"

"Ah, right. Then..." Ichijo reached inside the chest and pulled out the prize. "A piece of paper?" It was a rolled-up sheet of paper, tied with a ribbon.

"Could it be a treasure map?" someone asked.

"That must be it!"

Kageyama turned his face excitedly toward the murmuring students.

"I don't know precisely what the treasure is either," he confessed. "But I'm dying to see it! Please hurry and open it! Show it to everyone!"

"S-sure." Ichijo untied the ribbon and unfurled the sheet in a flourish so that everyone could see what was on it.

"What?"

The students looked up in shock at the paper. Written on it in beautiful calligraphy was a single word: Bonds.

"What's that supposed to mean?"

"It wasn't a treasure map then?"

The students turned confusedly to Headmaster Cross, who stood beaming proudly at them. He cleared his throat and explained. "As you can see," he began, "the treasure you searched for today was the bonds between all of you. Today you worked together, competed against one another, cried together, got angry together...The bonds of friendship you forge with people after going through these events together are treasures that you get to keep for all your lives. That's what I was trying to say!"

As soon as Headmaster Cross concluded his passionate speech, the students glanced at one another in confusion.

"Um..."

"Can I just ask...Why did we have to get kicked around by White Lily to form bonds?"

The atmosphere in the room grew gloomy. But up on the stage, Kageyama's eyes shined with tears as he applauded heartily. "That was beautiful, Headmaster Cross! Just magnificent! I love that my school is one in which we all can laugh together and help one another!"

Kageyama's reaction only made the general mood of the students worsen.

"Well, it wasn't a bad speech, but..."

"But yeah, it was kind of..."

"Hey, the mood in here is quickly souring," Yagari noted.

He glanced over at Kaito. As teachers they were meant to keep order, but just as they were about to get involved they heard something.

Clap, clap, clap, clap!

From somewhere in the midst of the crowd, someone had begun to clap. Everyone glanced around in confusion until they saw that it was Nadeshiko Shindo, the girl who had only just returned to the school that day.

Nadeshiko's face turned bright red at being the center of everyone's attention, but she declared bravely, "I thought it was magnificent too! Everyone, you had fun doing this treasure hunt, didn't you? It's been so long since we've all gotten excited over something like this. I just returned to Cross Academy today, and, to be honest, I had tried to come back once before. But that time this place was so sad that I couldn't do it. The school building was standing in ruins, and not all of my friends had returned either...This place had changed so much from the school I knew that I couldn't find the courage to come back."

The students stood quietly, listening to her.

"But you know what?" she continued, her face becoming more determined now. "When I came back today and participated in this treasure hunt, I had fun again! I laughed with my friends, ran around the campus with everyone...It's this kind of feeling that I truly missed from before. It's these kinds of times when you can make real memories. That's why I understand what the headmaster means about finding the treasure of the bonds that connect us."

The students were nodding in agreement.

"She's right. It has been a while since I've laughed as much as I did today."

"The missions were pretty fun in the end."

"It's been a while since I got to play around like this, so I guess it will be a good memory."

"Yeah, it's not so bad doing stuff like this once in a while."

From the stage Headmaster Cross saw the smiles on his students' faces and became rather teary-eyed. "All of you are such great kids! I'm so proud to have you as my students!"

"Thank you, Headmaster Cross! And you too, Kageyama!"

"Wait, why do I only get thanked after the headmaster?!" Kageyama demanded. "I did all the work!"

At Kageyama's protest, the entire crowd burst out laughing and cheering.

Against the wall, Kaito murmured, "Bonds, huh?"

Yagari turned his tender gaze from the stage to glance at his old student. "What's wrong, Kaito?"

Kaito shook his head. "Nothing. I was just thinking that it feels like I'd forgotten the importance of that word for a long time..."

"In times like these, it's easy to forget what's really important in life," said Yagari. "That's why we need to go out of our way to remind ourselves sometimes. That was probably why he wanted to do this." Yagari grinned. "That's so like him," he muttered fondly, then propelled himself from the wall to go outside for a cigarette.

After the treasure hunt there was a surprise barbeque party for the students that Headmaster Cross had secretly prepared. Under a sky aglow with the last rays of sunset, the students were allowed to cook up as much meat and vegetables as they liked on grills set up around the campus green. There were nothing but happy and contented faces all around.

"Yay! Meat!"

"After running all over the place, I've worked up a serious appetite!"

"It's a lot tastier eating it together with everyone, huh?"

Even the old Night Class members had come out to the lawn to watch the festivities.

"Akatsuki," said Ruka, "do you get the feeling there are more Night Class students now than there were earlier?"

"Well, it's close to sunset, so more of them have probably shown up now."

"There's still a long way to go in the outside world, but here at this school it looks like they really have come to coexist peacefully."

"I guess I don't hate it here..." was Shiki's endorsement.

Carrying a plate of barbequed meat, Kageyama came up to the group of aristocrats with the objective of talking to Ruka.

"R-Ruka," he stuttered. "If you'd like some barbeque, please feel free to have this." He presented the plate to her nervously. Ruka averted her face.

"No thank you. I don't find standing outside in the dirt while eating and trying to balance a plate of food in my hand appealing. Especially when I don't know who prepared it."

"Ruka! You don't remember me?"

"Um...Oh, that's right. You were the one hosting the treasure hunt earlier, weren't you?"

Kageyama was glad she had taken at least that much notice of him. But...

I guess that's really as far as my existence registers in her world, he thought. *Oh, Ruka...*

For a moment Kageyama's heart lamented silently. Unexpectedly, Kain reached out and squeezed his shoulder.

"Sorry about that," he said. "We know you worked hard to prepare that. I'll take it if you like?"

Just as he had on the night of the ball, Kageyama found himself following Kain's lead and handed him the plate.

"S-sure, go right ahead."

Disappointment remained on Kageyama's face, but a nearby group of students called out to him.

"Dorm President! Come join us!"

"We've got some meat fresh off the grill!"

Huh? Dorm president? Kain thought. Watching Kageyama's quick retreat to his group of friends, Kain suddenly remembered. *The push-up contest! It was held in his bedroom.* Kain had read the doorplate for the dormitory president's room as they had gone in to face Yagari. It meant that Ruka had been inside Kageyama's bedroom inadvertently that day. Kain grinned, but it wasn't the sort of thing one could chase after someone to say. So Kain just shrugged and continued eating his barbeque.

"This is actually pretty tasty," he said.

"Oh enough, Akatsuki," Ruka said. Her distaste was evident as she crossed her arms. Behind her, Rima was scanning the grounds.

"Where's Ichijo?"

"He's probably gone back to that place, I bet," Shiki muttered with a Pokkin Choco sticking out of his mouth.

*Back to the coffin of ice...*Shiki pictured his cousin asleep beneath the ice. After Kaname had taken his own heart and flung it into the furnace, Aido had thought fast and preserved his body in a block of ice. He knew Aido was not there tonight because he spent his every waking moment working to create his treatment for Kaname.

"Should we get going?" asked Kain.

"Yes, I'm ready to go," Ruka agreed. Shiki and Rima prepared to leave as well. There were things they all needed to do...

Nadeshiko greeted the head of the girls dormitory. "Thanks for taking care of me again this year," she said.

"Of course! Thanks for taking care of us as well, Shindo. By the way, you'll be sharing a room with Takizawa once again."

"What? With Maya?"

"Takizawa insisted that you would definitely come back someday, so we left your old bed open for you." The dorm president smiled at her.

"Oh, that Maya!" Nadeshiko cried. Wanting to laugh with delight, she set off in search of her best friend. As she circled the green, she encountered Sayori instead.

"Oh, Shindo!" said Sayori. "Thank you for what you said earlier. You really saved us!"

"Not at all," said Nadeshiko. "I just said what I felt in my heart. The only reason everyone understood my feelings was because of what you, Kageyama, and Headmaster Cross tried to show them."

Nadeshiko's cheeks reddened as she humbly brushed off her brave act. Just then, a teary-eyed Kageyama walked past them.

"Oh! Are you all right?" Sayori called out to him. Kageyama turned solemnly to the pair of them.

"Wakaba! Shindo! I swear I will return this academy to its former glory and bring the smiles back to everyone's faces! So please help me out again in the future!"

The girls exchanged a glance.

"I don't know what's happened to him, but he certainly looks fired up."

"True."

"I-in any case," Kageyama said hurriedly, "I really do appreciate your help!"

Nadeshiko and Sayori both stared at him blankly, but nodded in assent.

Making his way around the green as well was Kaito, who was continuing his role as cameraman by snapping photos of the students enjoying the barbeque.

"Hello there," Headmaster Cross greeted him. "Were you able to take lots of nice photographs today?"

"Yes, Headmaster," Kaito replied. "Plenty!"

Headmaster Cross beamed at him. He looked happy. "I'm truly glad we decided to do this today," he said. "I need to thank Kageyama for suggesting and planning this event."

"The students look refreshed," said Kaito, "and I'll bet this will give a boost to the general feeling on campus. You know, that speech you gave about bonds...It really surprised me."

"This school is going to be all right," said Headmaster Cross. "I'll protect all these smiles from now on. So Kaito, I hope you'll lend me your strength as well."

Students were scattered about the lawn enjoying the night. It seemed the Day Class and Night Class students were not quite ready to completely mingle together yet, but given more chances to see and get to know one another, Headmaster Cross knew the divisions would melt away in time.

Watching the students with the headmaster, Kaito suddenly raised his camera once again. "I guess it won't be so bad sticking around here," he said.

On a later day, Kageyama, Sayori, Kaito, and Nadeshiko had gathered to bury a new time capsule. This one contained the plans they had drawn up for their treasure hunt, photos of the event, various student works, memorable items left behind in the dorms by past students, and essays by current students about school memories. Happily there were as many items from the Night Class as there were from the Day Class.

With everything packed into the capsule, they were about to close the lid when Kageyama spoke up. "Wait just a moment, please." He reached into his pocket and pulled out a sheet of paper—an answer sheet from a test.

"Huh?"

Sayori's eyes grew round as she took in the name written on the sheet. It was one she knew very well.

"Yuki Cross...That's one of Yuki's tests? But where did you find it?" she asked.

"Under some books in the staff room."

Kaito chuckled. "Wow, it's covered in red marks!" He looked impressed at the sheer number of wrong answers.

"Um, this is actually one of Yuki's better scores," Sayori reported.

"You're joking!"

"No. And just look at the way she managed to triumph over her perpetual drowsiness to write in letters that didn't trail off into chicken scratch," Sayori said with a straight face. "This could be her greatest work on a test ever. A miracle."

Kageyama's glasses glinted and a large smirk appeared on his face. "Wouldn't it be funny if Yuki Cross wound up being the one to find this time capsule? She'd be so embarrassed..."

Placing the test sheet at the very top of the items in the chest, they closed the lid and locked it shut. Then Kaito and Kageyama lifted the chest and placed it into the hole they had prepared.

As Sayori watched them refill the hole with dirt, she murmured, "It would be great if Yuki really did find this time capsule someday."

Kaito paused to grin at her. "I bet she'd turn red and get really mad."

"She would," Sayori agreed. "But she'd get a good laugh out of it too."

"Who knows who will find it?" said Nadeshiko. "But whoever does, I hope we inspire them to put on an event like we did and that they have a wonderful time together." She sent these wishes silently into the capsule as well.

Having finished reburying it, Kageyama faced the mound covering the capsule, clasped his hands together, and bowed his head as though in prayer.

"Kageyama?" said Sayori. "What are you doing?"

With his eyes still closed Kageyama cried, "Friends forever! May all who pass through Cross Academy remain ever smiling! That is my one true wish."

"That is so lame."

"Mr. Takamiya! Please don't say such things!"

Kaito laughed. "I'm sorry. But you don't have to worry. I think everyone definitely heard your message loud and clear at the treasure hunt. I'm sure that someday more students will return to school here." He clasped Kageyama's shoulder.

The four looked over at the old school building where crews had begun work clearing the old wreckage. The rebirth of Cross Academy was under way.

Hi, everyone! It is I, Ayuna Fujisaki—she who finally achieved her five-year dream of wanting to write a story starring White Lily! I sure hope everyone enjoyed this *Vampire Knight* novel filled with Hino Sensei's beautiful illustrations! This time we were able to include six stories with six very different themes. It is quite a diverse book!

The Japanese word for "fleeting" in the novel's title *Fleeting Dreams* is a word we created using the kanji for "gleam" and "silver." The "silver" symbolizes Zero, and I added "gleam" for the transient image of when light hits silver. Thus, we combined them to mean "fleeting." Five of the stories talk about ways various characters "gleam" to document a fleeting emotion they had.

"A Maiden's Melancholy" is the only one that takes place while Yuki is still attending Cross Academy. The other five were placed chronologically as they occurred in the manga. I think readers will get some extra enjoyment if they match up the stories to where they fall in the manga timeline. Zero and Kaito visiting Dahlia Academy is one example of that. (Though the one that wound up surprising me most was finding out that Sara-sama's first love was you-know-who!)

Speaking of Kaito—he is now a regular character in the manga! (Talk about surprises!) To celebrate I made sure we had lots of him in this book too.

Changing the topic abruptly—let's talk about the last chapter of the manga. I cried so hard. My heart felt so full at the end, like we'd come to the conclusion of a long, grand journey. I am so grateful I encountered such an incredible series. As a genuine fan myself, I know I will continue to love *Vampire Knight* always.

–**Ayuna Fujisaki**, Autumn 2013

In this *Vampire Knight* novel you can see the skillful hand of Fujisaki-sama, who has taken both her ideas and my ideas and mixed them into one terrific, seamless whole. I am so happy to have gotten the chance to work with Fujisaki-sama on another novel. I feel like I had a huge grin on my face the whole time I was reading her finished work. I'm just so pleased. I really enjoyed drawing the illustrations for this novel as well!

But before I get too carried away in my happiness, there's something I mustn't forget to mention. While Fujisaki-sama was writing the drafts for the first two *Vampire Knight* novels, after I had reviewed them there were numerous times I had to tell our editor, "I'm so sorry, but this topic overlaps with something I wanted to cover in a future chapter of the manga." I had to request Fujisaki-sama to write something else. Now that the manga has ended, it turns out I didn't actually wind up including many of those topics. I feel like I've wronged her because of that.

There was no need to worry about overlaps for this novel, which was planned after all the material through the end of the manga had been decided. Fujisaki-sama was able to pick the topics she wanted. But seeing the topics made me feel so lonely. I wished I could have drawn more of these things in the manga myself. It's made me realize how much I've treasured the experience of creating *Vampire Knight*. On the other hand, I'm both extremely thrilled and anxious that some of the material I couldn't get to will come to light in this novel. The story of Sara and you-know-who never even surfaced in any of our editorial meetings during the manga's serialization...

I'm so happy Fujisaki-sama was willing to take on this project! She brought a great continuity to the six stories and gave my characters interesting new characters to meet and interact with as well. I'm truly grateful to her from the bottom of my heart. Thank you so much, Fujisaka-sama! My characters' "time spent outside the manga scenes" can really be found here. I'm just as happy to experience the joy of reading about those times as my readers.

—**Matsuri Hino**, Autumn 2013

Matsuri Hino

Birthday: January 24 | Hometown: Hokkaido

Matsuri Hino burst onto the manga scene with her title *Kono Yume ga Sametara* (When This Dream Is Over), which was published in *LaLa DX* magazine. Hino was a manga artist a mere nine months after she decided to become one.

With the success of her popular series *Captive Hearts* and *MeruPuri*, Hino has established herself as a major player in the world of shojo manga.

Hino enjoys creative activities and has commented that she would have been either an architect or an apprentice to traditional Japanese craft masters if she had not become a manga artist.

Ayuna Fujisaki

Birthday: July 14 | Hometown: Tokyo

Ayuna Fujisaki made her debut as an author in 1994. She worked on the staff of the *Vampire Knight* TV anime. Her blood type is the outgoing and carefree O.

Other works by
Matsuri Hino

Vampire Knight

The Art of Vampire Knight

Vampire Knight Official Fan Book

Wanted

MeruPuri

Captive Hearts

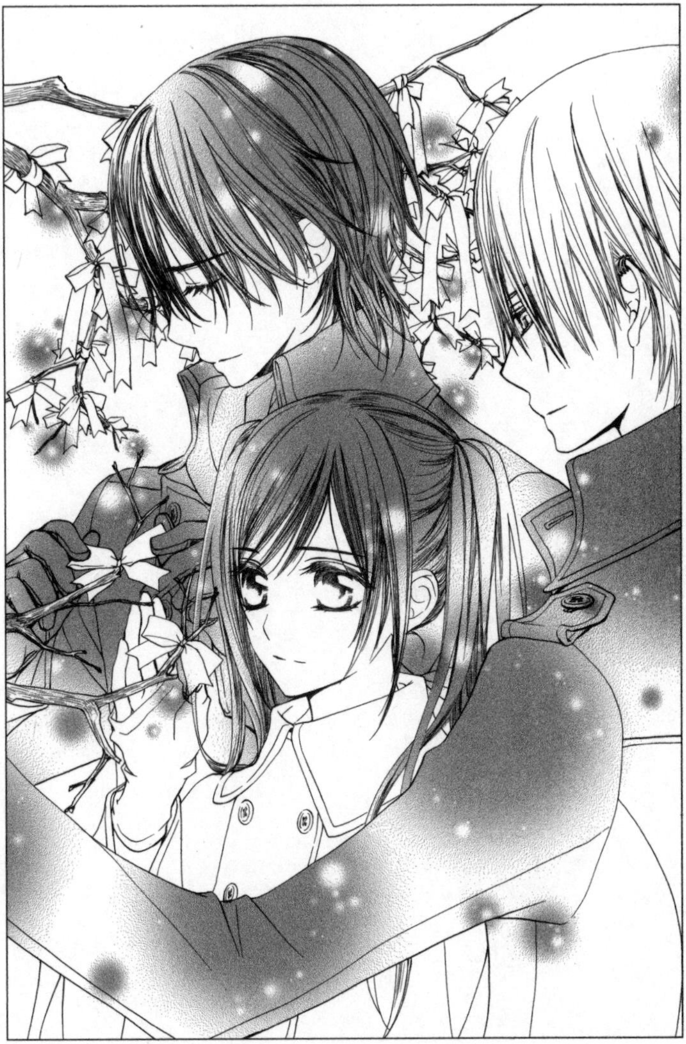